LESSONS FROM A GENTLEMAN

A Conversation regarding Love,
Sex, Dating and Relationships

Mike Anthony

authorHOUSE®

AuthorHouse™
1663 Liberty Drive
Bloomington, IN 47403
www.authorhouse.com
Phone: 1 (800) 839-8640

Published by AuthorHouse 05/31/2018

ISBN: 978-1-5462-4501-8 (sc)
ISBN: 978-1-5462-4499-8 (hc)
ISBN: 978-1-5462-4500-1 (e)

Library of Congress Control Number: 2018906531

Print information available on the last page.

Contents

From the Desk of the Author

Greetings,

I'm Michael Anthony Holland, from Oakland, Ca I'm the son of Charles A. Holland Sr. and Sharon M. Jarvis. Brother of Dwayne Holland, Charles Holland and Shawanna Emerson and the uncle of Kingston A. Holland and Tysean Jackson. I graduated from Skyline High School in Oakland, went on to attend Art Institute of Atlanta, where I studied Fashion & Retail management. I've always had a love for writing and find myself to be a student of life and love, so I felt it was only right that I pined my thoughts in a book. I host red carpet events under Plush Entertainment. In short, I love God, my family, my friends, those who have supported my journey in one way or another.

Special thanks and appreciation to God for making this all possible. My family for always being supportive in all my wild dreams. My friends for always being a support group and all of you for supporting. I pray that something I've written in this book will encourage you, challenge you and help you.

Introduction

The journey to find love isn't easy for any man, or woman for that fact. While there are still those who find love, many are still stand in their own way of experiencing true love. We as people are afraid of the unknown, especially us men. Its human nature for us to be afraid of what we can't see, that which we've never experienced, but to find or gain something you've never had, you must be willing to take the risk. Life has taught me to be patient when searching for love, someone to love. In a world where people want everything fast, quick and easy I believe that the more precious the gift, the more time and effort it takes to obtain and receive it. Ladies, it's my hope that by the end of this book you will have a better understanding of what to look out for when considering a husband, mate, a partner. Gentleman, I hope that you will be challenged to become your best self, If you're not walking in the light of what a gentleman represents, that you'll want to begin doing so. I hope that in my pain you find wisdom as I have. No, it's not easy, but I believe when you find the right one, it'll be worth it. Trust the process.

CHAPTER 1

"The Learning Curve"

There comes a time in every man's life where he finds himself at a cross road of mentally maturing or continuing to keep a child's frame of mind. Generally, the age at which this happens is between twenty-six and thirty-one. While this is the case for many, I hit this crossroad at the tinder age of nineteen. Imagine, here it is I'm nineteen and already I'm ready to find something real, I'm ready to stop playing games. You see where I'm from, that's not the most popular thing for a young African American man, or any man to be honest. Many men and women are about playing games, whether it's to keep from getting their heart broken or just out of neglect of respect for another person's time, effort and energy.

Unfortunately, I've come across many women who have been hurt; therefore, I caught the bad end of the stick and ended up getting hurt in an effort to love women who weren't able to love me back considering they had a broken heart. The desire to love someone is never a bad thing if they're available to be loved by you. Often, we want what we can't have, or even in some cases shouldn't have because they aren't who God intends for us to be with. I can't count how many times I've had someone with potential to be my wife because we clicked or because it felt right. Mind you, this is coming from a man who's been engaged twice already and not even thirty years old, but I'll get to that later. It gets discouraging at times of course I wonder will I ever actually experience true love.

Will I find my soulmate? Is she right in front of me and I'm too blind to see it? Let's face it; the closer we get to thirty, the more serious we begin to really take life, dating, relationships and love. I had to learn that while I am a gentleman, that's foreign on many levels in this day and age, so I can't expect for just any woman to understand or except the man that I am. I've learned that being a gentleman requires special patience because in most cases while we're being ourselves a lot of time is spent trying to show or convince a woman it's who we really are.

Now, I realize at this point some ladies may be thinking if so many men didn't play games it wouldn't be so difficult and while I agree, I also find the positive in that. For instance, it's those bad relationships that help us to appreciate the good ones; it's those experiences that have caused us pain that helps us to embrace the moments filled with joy. I understand that this doesn't justify bad behavior and believe me, in no way am I attempting to do so but

I am hoping this will help you begin to see things from a different point of view. It's in our experiences that we learn most about ourselves, rather than another person. We can't control someone else's actions, but we can control our reactions.

I've dealt with many situations and circumstances which could have caused me to become discouraged and could have caused me to turn away from finding love but instead of turning away, I grew, I've been resilient and I've grown to want it even more. Now, of course that's just me, not everyone will take heartache and disappointment and learn from it and want to grow even more, in fact, most will do the opposite. People shy away from love after experiencing heartache, after experiencing a bad relationship. This is the point at which we should take those experiences, allow them to teach us, become better and apply that which we've learned in our next relationship.

Imagine, if we all were to turn away from relationships, dating, love after a bad situation, we wouldn't be able to find a soul to mate with or a heart to love. There's someone who's looking for what you must offer, who will accept the good and the bad but if you give up before they have the ability to come around, you're not only cheating them, but you're cheating yourself.

It's in love that we discover our true selves. We're in our most vulnerable state mentally, physically and emotionally. Being in love is the biggest risk-taking investment that one can make. It's a decision to allow someone to gain access to our time, finances, heart, emotions, even our thoughts. This takes an act of faith, considering we don't know the end results, yet we believe that person is who they've presented to be, we believe that they are worth taking a risk, taking a chance on without a guarantee that they are in fact worth giving the opportunity to.

Both men and women take risk in the effort to find love. One of the most debatable arguments is that women love harder than men and as a man I'd have to say that it's not that women love harder but I do believe that women are more vulnerable while in love do to the overall makeup of a woman. This doesn't make a woman weak; it makes her a tad bit braver in love. Men are stand offish when it comes to being open to love, when it comes to allowing a woman to have our hearts totally, because we don't want to end up heartbroken or feeling as though our time has been wasted. I'm a person who doesn't mind spending money on the one I'm dating; I believe it's wise to invest in the person we're dating monetarily, emotionally, physically and most of all, spiritually. Many say put your money where your mouth is, I say, invest your money where your heart is. Money, we will get back, but time is the one thing that, once it's spent, it's gone forever and the next minute isn't promised.

As a youth I wasn't confident in who I was. Don't get me wrong, I wasn't ugly but I didn't display a level of confidence that would allude to a girl that I was a good catch. We have the ability to train people how they are to treat us by the way we treat ourselves. If we display a level of confidence in ourselves that exemplify we are different, we are a catch, that we have something special about us that they won't be able to find anywhere else, it causes that person or people to become interested in knowing exactly what that something, what that mystery is. I recall having my first girlfriend in the fifth grade by the name of Shante. Interesting enough, she was the finest girl at Sobrante Park Elementary School in Oakland and I had her. Of course, you could imagine the level of confidence this gave me at that time but little did I know this confidence would help me as I grew into the man I am today. I'm not one to brag, but I allow my work to prove my worth. Knowing what you have to offer is a key to attracting the right attention.

Not every person you meet will be the one, but always consider the law of attraction. The energy we put out in the world is the energy that will come into our lives. If you put out positive vibes and good energy regardless of whether or not you receive it immediately, know that it will happen when the time is right.

I often tell people that love is the one thing is life we'll get wrong ninety-nine percent of the time but the one time we get it right overrides all the times we got it wrong. Just as any situation or circumstance in life leaves us with choices on whether we weather the storm or give up. Often we find ourselves giving up because we haven't received what we're expecting, when we expected it, often times causing us to miss out on a good thing just before we get it. The struggle is designed to build us up so when we finally do get that significant other, we don't take it for granted. No one wants to feel as though they've been taken for granted or that their efforts aren't good enough. We all have the ability of making someone feel special, we just must take the time to learn that person. There are instances where we don't realize that a person is giving us their all simply because their effort is different from what we feel it should be.

I would venture to say that many people in the world today don't understand the concept of loving someone whole heartedly. Most people love the idea of being in love, having that special someone to call their own but when they realize it's more than just posting nice photos on Instagram and making her your WCW or making him your MCM they question themselves as to whether or not they're really ready to experience love. The interesting concept of being in love is realizing that in many cases we become unselfish. We tend to put that special someone before ourselves which while this is a beautiful thing, it's also important to make sure that we don't lose ourselves inside of the relationship.

Only you can make yourself happy, others are able to add happiness to your life but the initial point of happiness begins with self. We often expect happiness to come from others never realizing that we have the ability to make ourselves happy. Knowing what makes you happy and doing what makes you happy is important before finding or searching for love. I oftentimes hear women say he made me happy or they make me happy and oftentimes I question them asking, well what happens when they stop doing what they do to make you happy? Do you become sad? Do you become depressed?

Oftentimes the words we speak create our reality without us even realizing that what we were afraid of is exactly what we created or caused to exist in our world.

There comes a time in every man's life where what we've learned, whether by our surroundings, teachings or experiences is put to the test and we're left with the options of actually becoming better or becoming bitter.

The lesson I believe we can all learn is that, love is not a game, love isn't something we play. People's time, hearts, energy, shouldn't be played on. Take a moment and think about the many times you've experienced the game. Whether you were the one playing them or if you were the one being played with. Time is the one gift in life we get that once it is spent, we can't get it back, so why waste it? Why is it that we take it for granted? I've been in a situation where I pursued a woman, who started out being my friend, then we became best friends, mind you I'm talking about going back as far as pre-teen years. The interesting fact is that, I knew of her, but I didn't really begin to have feelings for her until we began to open up to one another, this gave me the actual chance of knowing her. When I decided to take a chance on taking that friendship to the next level, thinking we were on the same page, it turned out we weren't on the same page, which I'm sure you can imagine hurt, brought about a unrepairable broken friendship. I invested my time, energy, effort, support, love, care, trust, you name it, I invested it all into this friendship, for years.

The point I'm trying to make is that, had she let me know from the beginning, it wasn't going anywhere, we could have salvaged that friendship. Instead, I ended up feeling, hurt, ashamed, embarrassed, I mean, it's not like it was a secret how I felt about her. Knowing the dating game, how it is in today's society, this time, I didn't even think to play it, not with her and you know what they say, *"Nice guys finish last,"* well, I'm living proof of that harsh reality. Being a gentleman requires a lot and the risk are high, if it weren't so, many men wouldn't choose to be what's known as the *"F-boy"*, which we will get into this special type of male species a bit later. Ultimately, being a gentleman is a choice of going against what everyone else says or thinks and solely focusing in on the bigger picture, for me, that bigger picture was marriage. I decided, if I'm going to pursue, it's not just for a moment, it's for a lifetime of moments.

The lesson, being the most difficult I've had to learn was the importance of knowing when to tap out vs knowing when to go harder. Now, I know what you're thinking fellas, if she's playing games, I'm tapping out quick. While that sounds easy, there comes a time in every man's life where he meets, come across or realizes that he's entertaining a woman who's far different from the rest and you know this when you find yourself reasoning in the sensitive areas that you normally wouldn't reason in. You're a business man, therefore, you think business even when dating. Well, if you're in your dream career and things aren't what you expected, do you throw in the towel and quit? No, you look for solutions, implement changes and come back and try again, hoping for a different outcome. Not You?

Ok, how about this one, you're about your money, therefore you invest, whether it's for additional income, building your savings or planning for the future, in any investment you're expecting or hoping for a return on that investment and just like the market is unpredictable, people, women especially are even more unpredictable. If your return on investment isn't what you expect it to be, in most cases you hope to break even, at least but the truth of the matter is, that's no guarantee, yet, you continue investing right? Perhaps, if you are wise enough, not in the same stock or what many are investing in now and days known as crypto currency, instead, you invest elsewhere.

The question I'm left with is, why when something doesn't work out with one woman, do we shut Love or even the idea of love off? Yes, I get it, trust me, we as men, don't like feeling vulnerable, open to being hurt, trusting someone with access to our emotions and in love, all of these, plus many others are experienced. The right woman, or man, ladies, shouldn't have to suffer for all the wrong one's mistakes. In no way, shape, form or fashion am I suggesting just open to any or every person that enters your life, but I am challenging you, along with myself, to be open to allowing a genuine connection to take place and see where it leads. The right one could be the next one, but you'll never know unless you're willing to take the risk, have faith and believe love, true love exist.

Many people give up on love, relationships, even dreams before they get their breakthrough, not realizing how close they were to receiving it. You never know how close you are to receiving until you receive it. Ladies, that man could be watching you, observing how you move, how you interact, how you treat yourself and others and soon as he's ready to step up to the plate, you let yourself go. You stop keeping your hair done, or putting a hat on if it's not done, you've stopped smiling, you walk around mean mugging people as though you are unhappy and just as you don't want a miserable man in your life, no man wants a miserable woman in theirs. Most men watch before they pursue. Some, like myself, will observe on multiple occasions to see if the person we seen, that caught our eye, is really who you are, or did we just catch you on an extremely good day.

CHAPTER 2

"Going Hard Vs Going Home"

We live in a day and age where people are so quick to jump ship at the first sign of trouble. Now don't get me wrong I'm not saying ignore the red flags however think for a minute ask yourself is this something that we can work on? Is this baggage that I'm going to carry? We all have our baggage, let's face it nobody's perfect, however we all have a choice in the matter. We have a choice whether we are willing to hang in there when times get difficult. There comes a time in every relationship where things get real, a time where you find yourself questioning everything that goes on in the relationship. You begin to ask yourself, is this something serious? Can I really see myself with this person in the future? Believe it or not this is the point where most relationships are broken, even before a physical breakup there's a mental break up that happens. There's a point that men and women find themselves asking the same questions, Is this serious?

Is this someone I could see myself building a future with? Interesting enough, this is often the place in the relationship where men do something faulty and women start pushing a man away by way of pressuring him to commit.

We are often times tested in our relationships, not realizing that, a test is really all it is. We all are familiar with the obvious things we are tested with inside a relationship, those that we spark and those things that are sparked from outside sources. Cheating, lying, not getting along, having nothing in common to keep each other interested are among some of the top obvious reasons why many breakups are caused. For a moment, lets think about some of the others that often times get put on the back burner as reasons why people breakup.

Communication, is key to all understanding anyone and anything in this life. If we don't take time to understand a person chances are there will be a void and chaos in the relationship, triggered by this one element. Understanding your partner is key to knowing what they want, what the desire, also those things that will cause conflict in a relationship. I often wonder why is it that causes people to nitpick at those things they know will get under their partners skin and irritate them.

Being in a relationship should always cause you to flourish as a person. A healthy relationship will cause you to grow into the man or woman God designed you to be. With that person we become greater, not saying in any way that a single person can't be or isn't great, however I am saying having someone to grow with, learn with, travel with, earn with, learn from and even teach, adds to the value of life we live. Many times, we consider the times we get something wrong, but in love the one time we get it right cancels all the times we get it wrong. I've had many great relationships that contributed to the overall wellbeing of the man I am today.

Many relationships we encounter are meant to teach us lessons and prepare us for the person God intends for us to be with. Don't mistake your lessons for lifetime experiences, know when to say thank you and move on with life. It's always wise to consider what you're losing by walking away? Is it something that they've imparted in your life that you can't find anywhere else? Did God himself speak to you regarding that person, or better yet, did you talk to God about them? We tend to put ourselves in situations that will lead us nowhere fast. I've learned that the best way to ensure this doesn't happen, is to be honest with yourself and with the person you're pursuing.

It's easy to quit, to walk away when we're tested in our relationships, with the help of social media many women have men thirsting in their dm's and men are quick to go hop in some woman's dm's. Being in a relationship requires extreme discipline, especially now and days where it seems options are literally at our finger tips. For men, while we don't require as much as women do, it doesn't take much for most to lose focus on who, what matters. Sticking with the one God intends for you to be with, will always be more beneficial than attempting to create something better with someone you think is better, just because things get tough. Love matters and means most in the worst of times.

Divorce is at an alarming rate for many different reasons. I believe we've put a time on love, which we shouldn't do. Love doesn't operate on our timing. Love operates on its own timing and when we understand that, we'll begin to become more patient with finding love and work harder at keeping it. Think about your last break up. What was the cause of it? What could you have don't to prevent it? Was it all their fault? What part did you play in it?

Many will quickly put the fault on the other person, especially and rightfully so, in most cases women. Maturity says, yes, I realize they may have done this or that, but I take responsibility for my actions as well. This is the ultimate sign of maturity and if we put this into practice while in our relationships, whether it's dating, professional or friendships, we'll find that many times what causes the problems are the build ups of recurring situations that we neglect to talk about. Sweeping things under the rug doesn't make them go away. When something goes wrong or is wrong in the relationship, it's important to bring that issue to the forefront. Communication is key to all understanding, and without understanding we can never find a solution. Are all things repairable? If you both want it bad enough, but a relationship on its own is work, with no days off, a relationship with problems requires overtime.

We must recognize there's a prize at the end of the

journey, bigger than ourselves, our own selfish desires. Think back to what caused you to pursue them in the first place, recall the moments you couldn't just look into each other's eyes but you stared. The role of a gentleman isn't to be perfect, but it's to show the true nature of what it means to make that special someone feel like she's that special someone, every chance you get. Sounds crazy, right? Well, it's very much so possible regardless of how long you've been with them. The good morning text, random checkups, making sure they've eaten throughout the day, opening the doors for her, random moments of spontaneity are all characteristics of being a gentleman. Many today will say that's cliché, or a display of thirst, but to one who is woke, she will be appreciative and even reciprocate in ways of queen like behavior.

Keeping the fire inside the relationships is the responsibility of both men and women. Many will argue it's up to the man, because he's the leader in the relationship, however men need to have actions reciprocated as well. You don't just drive your car without putting gas in the tank, do you? Just as a gas fills a car, appreciation shown to a man for his actions fills his fire and desire to continue doing kind gestures and even do more. I'm one who's a giver at heart. Many who know me will tell you this is truth, however, even I've gotten burned out after giving so much and not receiving anything in return. While a simple *"thank you"* is good and while it says appreciation, showing appreciation takes actions and as the saying goes "actions speak louder than words". Imagine being with someone who's unappreciative so much so, they fail to say thank you. For many, the first time, will cause you to say hmmm, that's interesting, perhaps they forgot or maybe they just missed it? The second time this occurs, it's more so of a done deal, a wrap. Nobody likes to feel Un-appreciated, whether they voice it or not. Men often times more than women are likely to show our disappointment by our actions, most simply shut down, some huff and puff, some become distant, regardless of what the action is, it speaks volumes.

Women on the other hand, tend to be more vocal when they feel any kind of way, good or bad, happy or sad, disappointed, upset, you name it. As men, we have to become more aware of our woman's actions, pay attention and show we actually care about the way she feels, grant it, some can be very minute to us, but at the end of the day, even the smallest occurrences, that seem to matter a lot to her, have to become important to you, not because the actual occurrence is important, but because she's important and because she's important to you, her passions, desires, hurts, pains, struggles, stresses whether big or small become just as important to you. Imagine, the time you'll save on heated debates, arguments, nagging, if you operated in this amount of care.

Now ladies, I know some of you seen one word in that entire sentence and felt some type of way, allow me to explain. Nagging when men refer to it often, is based on the tone that you use while trying to convey information or get your point across. Many of my friends who are married, use this term mostly. *"She's always nagging"* is a popular phrase that I believe has been around for decades now, mainly because, well, some women, choose to talk at a man vs to him, therefore causing her to be a nag. Not every woman falls in this category and don't get me wrong, I understand that there are times when us men, do things to cause women to become upset and in the midst of being upset, they express themselves in an aggressive tone. Most cases of this is caused by the repeating of a situation, talk, or action that a man does or continues to do without showing any signs of improvement.

Now gentlemen, we must become more conscious of our actions, especially those we know our woman don't appreciate or like us doing. Don't give her a reason to have the same talks, regarding the same things and you'll notice a more peaceful environment. Women don't just nag just because it's the thing to do, especially if you have a good woman. Understand, that a good woman comes with certain requirements, high standards, which will ultimately cause you to become a better man. The right woman can see into the man you were created to be, so often, it will be difficult, you won't understand why she's "over reacting" when in all actuality she's doing what a queen does, seeing to it that her king is at his best, at all times. The question of why a person does what they do, can often bring a better understanding of why they react the way they react.

We've all heard the phrase *"Go Hard or Go Home"* often

times referred to when mentioning a competitive sport. Applying this principle to our dating life will help us not cheat ourselves or the person we're courting, yes, I said courting. Listen, I have a saying,

"We date to find, we court to marry"

When dating someone, you're getting to know them, with the intent, hopefully of seeing if anything can be developed beyond that point. Often times while in this stage, you're entertaining other candidates who also fit your description of what you're looking for, or think you want. As we've all experienced in dating, especially in this generation of *"Ghosting"*, for those of you who shy away from social media outlets and social events, you may not be aware of this term, so for educational purposes, let me explain what that is. *"Ghosting"* is the act of talking to or getting to know someone, things could potentially be just fine, the vibe can be right, a possible connection could be blossoming into something genuine, but all of the sudden, they seem to start texting you less and less, responses become slower, call backs aren't a guarantee, then before you know it, they become obsolete in your life.

So, in dating, people come and go, in most cases, they have a way of removing themselves, then there are those who seem to be right often on paper, yet in reality, they lack in areas that are of significant value to us. While we're here, lets dive a bit into the way our society has caused us to want or be attracted to what's fake vs what's real, mainly because what's fake gets attention and what's real, often seems to be low key and overlooked. Women often times chose the guy with a certain level of status vs a guy who possess substance. Status, often blind women from seeing the reality of who a man really is behind closed doors. Substance, is often times hidden and only displayed when necessary or warranted. So, here it is, *"Nice guys finish last"* which I've heard throughout my entire life, because I've been marked as the nice guy, sometimes too nice but while I could've, maybe in some instances, should've displayed the not so nice guy attitude, that's just not me.

I strive to have a heart after God's therefor, in spite of how taken for granted I may be in some people's lives, I won't dump down my dopeness to make them feel comfortable. Anyone who wishes to be in your life should add to it, not be causing you to display mediocre behavior to make them feel comfortable about themselves. Yes, nice guys, do get overlooked, more often than they should, but funny enough, after a woman gets to a certain point in her life and begin to consider things that matter, they end up circling back around to the nice guys. We will go into more depth a little later, for now, allow me to challenge you to going hard in spite of what society calls thirsty or tries to downplay as being whipped. This goes for both men and women.

"People with opinions, will never trade their regrets for yours".

Can you think of someone who listened to the opinions of others and now, whether they admit it or not, have regrets? Perhaps, maybe even you have regrets for not allowing yourself to trust yourself, even when you felt how strong, beautiful, genuine a connection with someone was. Well, we all have slight regrets, although people love to quote they don't, trust me, just like I do, just like you do, they do as well. The world we live in has caused us to be so afraid to be vulnerable, to allow or trust someone to actually love us.

I can still be living my best life, knowing I've done something in my past that I regret. Having regrets help keeps you humble. I can think of a time that I was dating this young lady and it was fresh, new, she was fine, played basketball and had all these great qualities. The woman I dated prior to her came back around and because I was familiar with her and I was used to her, it was easy for me to revert backwards. I regretted that decision after going back. I knew that I missed out on something good with this new and fresh relationship. No, I don't still hold that regret, I grew and matured and learned from that mistake and that's what life is about, learning and growing.

CHAPTER 3

"The Hopeless Romantic"

The urban dictionary describes Hopeless Romantic as, "True, caring, and loving people. They are not made for today's standards", sadly. They believe in passion, chivalry, and true love. They have loved sincerely at one pointing their life, discovered what feels like, and can't understand why it was not returned in the same form. Hopeless Romantics are usually dreamers, idealists, and sincere, however what they expect in any relationship is a full return for their effort and caring, to be loved as much as they loved. What makes them "helpless" is the fact that they are few and far between in today's daily life, and usually get let down in the long run, even though they gave all the had to give, money, love, time, housing, belongings. Hopeless Romantics give 100% all the time, and hope for the same in return."

Ladies, let me take you on a mental journey, if you will. Close your eyes and picture this, a man who sees you the way God himself sees you, who denies himself of his own desires and considers you first, in fact, after pleasing God and doing his work, you are the only person on this earth he's intentionally aiming to please. This man, he will go out his way just to see you smile, he doesn't need anything, yet he will make up something, just to spend time with you, steal a moment with you. Imagine, because he knows you as God knows you, he's able to please you in ways, no man has ever been able to please you, a kiss from him, equates to that of sex with other men when considering how pleasurable it is. This man touches you deep, when he grabs you, you feel his strength, warmth, protection, yet you feel his compassion and how much he wants you and only you. When he looks at you, he doesn't just give an empty stare, but he gazes into your eyes as though he's navigating his way into your soul. He doesn't buy gifts because you can't get them yourself, nor does he buy gifts because he's apologetic for some dumb sh** he's done, but instead, because you're always on his mind, even when you probably shouldn't be, when he's out and see's something that he knows is your caliber, he sees you in it, wearing it, and him imagining you in it pleases and excites him so much, he's compelled to buy it for you. Although, it's a gift for you, it's a bigger gift for him.

Now, I imagine many of you by now are thinking or asking **"Where are they at"?** Well, they're in most cases closer than you think. I've been that guy to one woman in particular, we'll say her name is **"shawty"** at least, I desired to be that man to her fully but for reasons outside of my control, it never happened, she never allowed me to be that man. I was that guy and guess where it landed me? Lol Yep, you guessed it, smack dab in the friend zone. At least she tried, but I'm more of the all or nothing type of guy, especially when I've invested much into someone or something. In my case, I went hard and still ended up at home.

Well, it's not all on her. I knew what I was getting myself into even prior to pursuing, yet I felt she was worth the wait, the struggle, so I continued to pursue, until I was faced with reality that, she'll never see me in any other light than that of a friend. Hurt? You can believe it, I mean, she had been my friend, best friend, one I told all my secrets, fears, dreams to, the one I called anytime something good or bad happened in my life, the one I was hoping to grow with. The one who I trusted with my life, my time, my energy, my care, my love. I mean, I was ring in hand, or drawer, I should say, ready. Since then, I've tried to be that guy with other women, but they either weren't deserving of it, from me at least, or the connection wasn't strong enough for me to even want to show myself, who I truly was.

I said all that to say, ladies, sometimes, that guy you know wants more than a friendship from you, and for whatever reason you're hesitant, nervous, worried, afraid of losing that friendship or he doesn't fall within your parameters of what your *"type"* is, is worth taking a look into, a risk on because you'll never know exactly what all he has planned in the back of his mind for you, that will add to you, your life, that will cause you to flourish beyond the normal, that will enrich your life. The truth be told, the woman I'm speaking of may never read this, I kind of hope not, to be honest, I've said a mouth full but if she does, it'll probably be the first she hears about me planning on proposing to her, unless God works a miracle before then. *"Sheesh"*

The hopeless romantic has a stigma of being some sort of bad thing, which I hate because someone has to keep hope regarding love, for if hope dies, love also dies. Now, I always argue the fact that its normal for women to be hopeless romantics vs men to be, just as I argue I don't believe women love harder than men, but I do believe women are more prone to allowing themselves to love than men, but when a man loves, I mean, truly loves a woman, the debt of how deep his love goes can't be measured.

What if people who got married to one another were hopeless romantics? Do you think the divorce rate would be so high? Hmnnn perhaps? But I highly doubt it. Perhaps I have been a hopeless romantic in my past, but after many let downs, I've grown to give what I receive until a person proves their worth first. While my mind is always thinking of fresh new ideas for how to go about loving a woman, how to make her day, I've applied the golden principle "do unto others, as you would have them do unto you" and subtracted what I do from that, just to be safe. It's using wisdom in an effort to preserve and protect your heart.

Being a hopeless romantic isn't a bad thing, it's a beautiful thing, but you have to learn to make use wisdom over deciding and doing things based on what your heart feels. In life, they key element to learn, in all things, regardless of what they are, is balance. Having balance in life keeps you leveled, focused, humble yet confident, which are all key elements to overall success.

My mentor told me he pursued his wife for two years prior to even getting one date. When a man knows, he knows and he will do anything to put himself in position to make you his wife. Any man pursuing a woman, actively, with the right motive, if he gets her, he will do what it takes to keep her. Just as my mentor has done. He and his wife have been married for 25 years now and the way he talks about her, would make you think, they had just met, just fallen in love. His excitement, the way he misses her, I've never seen any married man too excited to talk to, get home to, spend time with, make plans with his wife and that's something I've prayed to experience as well when I do get married.

Perhaps my thinking is a bit out there, but I'm a firm believer that supernatural power takes place when you connect with someone who only wants what's best for you, sees the best in you, wants nothing from you but to see you excel in life to the best of your ability. Imagine connecting with someone who's able to tap into that inner you, that nobody else knows, not even you see it at times, but they're constantly pulling the best out of you, whether it's a struggle to get you to go with the flow or it's an easy process, whatever the case, it's nothing like having that special someone who feels you are worth going to battle for.

A gentleman operates in the mindset, ***"The fact that I'm still alive, chivalry can't be dead"***. That's one of the principles I've lived by and what has caused me to hold myself as a man, to a higher standard. When we begin to change our mindset regarding ourselves, realizing no matter what our background is, no matter what we've been through or may even be going through currently, that our situation doesn't define who we are. We can control the way our book ends. The things we encounter in this life, often time, exist without our permission, while we can't control the things that happen, we do have the ability to control the way we react to them. A person who chooses to be upset, angry or depressed, is making a conscious decision based on what they're currently going through to put their energy into being depressed rather than choosing to fight, get help, step up to the plate and swing for the stars. My challenge is that you'll begin to discover those hidden truths about yourself and dive into them.

> ***"The many things we are ignorant to in this life, to die and be ignorant regarding ourselves, would be the worse tragedy"***

When we know ourselves, we know our love language, we know the things that makes us happy, sad, those things that piss us off, make us mad, therefor we're able to navigate through life, purposely avoiding things and people who mean us no good. Had I known then what I know now, I would've, should've, could've avoided some things, I would've done more, I could've loved more.

Don't allow your life to be filled with should've, could've, would've moments, the charge of your life, what you want, what you desire and work until they become a reality. While, the phrase "Hopeless Romantic" is often mentioned as though that person has some sort of disorder, I believe a hopeless romantic is anything but hopeless, too me, it seems as though they're more hopeful that anything. It's important to ensure you're not being taken advantage of, not being taken for granted because that's what causes many hopeless romantics to come discouraged and afraid to love again. We face obstacles of what society tries to portray and push off on us regarding how they believe or feel people who love or are in love should behave.

A gentleman knows there are limits at which he should invest in a woman vs his woman. Yes, it matters a great ideal. I've done many things for women I've dated, from taking them out in limousines, nice restaurants, creating dates out of the blue, whether it's a lunch date at the lake or a nice park, going to the beach, concerts with some pretty amazing seats, whether on the floor or in executive suites, but nothing I've done tops the things I have planned for my wife. I'm a hopeless romantic, at heart and with the right person, in action. I love to create experiences for my queen. Let me share my own personal experience with you all.

"Don't Judge Me"

Listen, *"shawty"* was my queen and you couldn't tell me anything different, we were connected spiritually to the point where without talking to one another on certain days, we'd know exactly what the other needed prayer for, emotionally to the point where if I were experiencing chest pains, she'd feel it, physically to the point where, kissing her, was more pleasurable that sex I had with other women. Yep, like *"Bruce Leeroy"* from the movie *"Last Dragon"*, she had the glow. Lol I had done things for her that people called me crazy for doing. Married men would tell me *"mannn, I don't even do that for my wife"* and yet, to me, what I had done, were considered to be investments because I had my eyes set on the ultimate goal, the final prize bring marriage. Now, did things pan out the way I had hoped and dreamed, No, but I hope that what I imparted in her life will lead her to knowing real, when she feels it.

There were things I had planned on doing, that looking back, I'm glad that I didn't do, reason being is, some things I only want to experience with my wife, the one I say*"I Do"* to. So, while many may look and think I did a lot, to me, because I know all the plans I actually have in the future, I don't think so. Ladies and Gents, it's important that whatever you do, you do because you genuinely want too and most of all, do things with the right motive in mind. Do you want basic? Or do you want extraordinaire? Well, whether you're classified as a *"Hopeless Romantic"* or not, hopefully, you want extraordinaire, especially when you know it's available to you. The basic is normal and for many, there's nothing wrong with the norm, but If you can work for the A grade, why settle for the C.

So often we settle for what seems to be right vs going after what, or who is right. If you're wondering how to tell the difference between the two, time is a relationships best tester. To go through a series of events, both good and bad, often times now and days, people are quick to walk away vs stand and fight to make things better, make things work. Those who choose to settle often times set themselves up for divorce in the long run, or short run even. What's temporary doesn't last, that's why its temporary, so why is it when we know something, someone, or a situation is temporary do we try to force it into the lifetime category? Is it because we feel we're racing against father time? Is it because we see we're pressured by what our family says, society tries to pressure us to believing we should be at a certain stage in life at a certain point in life?

Whatever the case is, don't allow people to put their time stamp on your life, especially if it doesn't concern them. Ladies, I hear you thinking, *"Well, I'm not about to wait for him to propose or take our relationship to the next level"* and you know what I say *"don't"*. There's a difference in a man who's not ready, yet working to get ready, then a man who's just not ready with no intent on getting ready or prepared for marriage. There's no such thing as the perfect time, yes, timing is everything, however, if we solely operate on that principle, that excludes the use of us needing to have faith in some areas. Sometimes, the perfect time is when you create the time.

CHAPTER 4

*"The F*** Boy"*

As I sit here writing this chapter, I find myself laughing because, sadly, many will read this chapter first, before the previous three. This phrase describes a man that many women have become well acquainted with, unfortunately. The truth is, *F**** boys weren't born that way, they've become that over their lifetime, whether the cause of it was due to the way they were brought up, things they've seen, or experiences they've had with a woman. Eyes will probably begin to roll when I say this, but I don't blame the *f**** boy for causing a woman to get hurt, no, I don't blame the woman either, however I will say, people will only do what we allow. In most cases women know a *f**** boy when they see one or meet one, yet most of them today, have the swag that most, many women want. So, women allow their eyes to lead them into a path that ultimately leads to them being disappointed, mad, angry, hurt, all because they based their getting to know him off of his looks and what he presents materialistically. *"Ouch"* I know, it hurts, truth has an interesting sting to it.

The *"F"* boy is only concerned with himself, he runs game, plays games, some, so well that only time has a way of showing his true intentions, if he's experienced, that is. The *"f"* boy's intentions are primarily to have sex, hit it and quit it, toot it and boot it. Yes, he may keep you around, but even then, that's only until he gets tired of you or find something better, someone different. While he has the swagger like Mcjagger and while, he may provide you with a sense of some sort of sensation, or feel good moments, it's important to get to know him, slowly. You have to realize that, often time, people, especially, many men will rush to get you involved in something, that they don't intend on going anywhere fast. Men of this caliber will do what it takes to get what they want and once they do, you will notice a slight change in interaction. All of the sudden, they're busy, when they use to answer on first or second ring, now you get the auto-reply text message. They used to take you out on dates, now most time is spent at his place or yours, Netflix and Chill has become your regular Friday night.

I get it, this generation is easily impressed by the glitz and glam. We've lost focus of values and character. Forget about what seems legit, things now and days are hardly ever what they seem. The sad reality is that these gentlemen aren't at fault.

Yep, I said it, they're only playing the game that society has dictated has to be played in order to win.

Think about it, why is it that, "*f*" boys and "hoes" get wifed up or get the most action in the dating scene? Many women swear up and down they want something real, but when real approaches, you don't sense that "*f*" boy vibe, so instead you make up excuses for why you won't give him the opportunity to get to know you. He's too nice, he's too sweet, he's such a gentleman, he's a great friend, he's my best friend. Yet, when the "*f*" boy approaches your eyes light up, because he gives off that vibe that he'll do you wrong, and deep down, women like that. Women are natural nurturers, which often times lead them to becoming natural fixers. Ladies, a man is one project that no matter how much time you spend trying to fix or change, he won't change, unless he himself, decides within his heart that he's ready and wants to change.

In no way am I saying you're a bad woman for wanting to connect with a certain man and put the effort in to make the relationship work with him, given, he's putting in the effort to make it work with you also. Sometimes, you have to know when to let him go, realize, rather or not you were playing the game as well, the fact that he was, he accomplished his goal and now, there's nothing left to give. The "*f*" boy doesn't just have a certain look, and there are many different classifications that will cause for a man to be put into this category. You can't specify a "*f*" boy to a certain job, career, look. The one thing "*f*" boys have in common are their mentalities.

What's that? Ladies, I hear you thinking. Well, here's

the secret, that I'll probably lose my player card for telling. The goal is to get in before you realize they're only playing games with you and get out before catching feelings for you. Anytime a man is moving in a fast pace, that's something you should always be cautious of. That is a red flag. The more time we spend outside on dates, that will speed up the process of the time, we get to spend inside, your bed.

While you may be enjoying reading this segment so far ladies, there is one thing, one type of person that's worse than a "*f*" boy, you know what that is? A "*f*" girl. Yes, I'm going there. It's no secret that the game has changed, dating has changed. We're no longer in the old school way of doing things and women are so independent that often, they feel don't need a man for anything outside of sex, even then, most keep Mr. West In the panty drawer to the left. The "*f*" girl has the same type of heart as the "*f*" boy and they're able to be successful at being a "*f*" girl because the amount of thirst they receive in their DM's on IG or Facebook, or in public.

These women are typically cute, but more so, men find them to be sexy, thick, fat a**, nice titts, face doesn't have to be a ten, but the body normally is. These women, play the game so well that you would think they are wholesome, church going, educated, kind hearted, respectable women, at least they appear to be, but deep down, they're just as shady and self-centered as the "*f*" boy. They only care about what a man can do for them. They tend to make you feel as though you're the one, when there are about five other guys who feel the same way. Ladies, am I lying?

Now fellas, just as they can't put every "*f*" boy in a certain category, we can't put them in a certain category. These women are everywhere, not just where you'd expect them to be. They're in your local shopping malls of course, at the Macy's makeup counter, Club, lounges, Bars, Church, Gym, pretty much everywhere you are, you have the potential of running into a "*f*" girl. You will be tempted to holler at her, but if you're looking for something real, substantial, that will lead to something great in the long run, I encourage you to look but don't even engage. Save yourself, your time, energy and money. Those are the three things they will take from you, your time, energy and money. I often time see on IG a quote "A bad *B**ch* is a bill, a good woman is an investment" I couldn't agree with this anymore.

I recall a conversation I had with a good friend of mine, George. George is a business owner and married for quite some time with kids. He stated, "Mike, whatever you do, make sure you marry the right woman. When you marry the right woman, life begins again, when you marry the wrong woman, life ends". I understand exactly what he's saying, when you marry the right woman, she has a way of actually giving to you, adding to you, enhancing your life. A good woman to a man is like makeup applied to a beautiful woman. It doesn't change you, but it adds to you, it enhances your life. Find someone who's reliable, accountable, dependable, who make themselves available for you. The most precious gift we're given in this life, is time. It's the one thing that once it's spent, you can't retrieve. If you want to know who you're important to, just think about who makes time for you, who tries to spend time with you. Perhaps you also want to look at those who you give your time too. Not everyone is worth your time, energy and effort. You can be friends with a person your whole life, but that doesn't mean they're meant to stay in your life. Knowing when to let go, will prevent you from feeling like your time has been wasted. It's not the easiest thing to do, but it's necessary.

"Wasting Ten years, Is Better than Wasting Eleven"

So, how do we go about making sure we're not entertaining "f" boys and girls? Better yet, how do we go about ensuring we aren't labeled as or fall under the category of one? Self-reflection time on a daily or weekly basis can ensure we don't slip into this category. Work on self, to constantly get better, become better in every area of your life. If you spend time working on yourself, you don't have time to be in everyone else's business.

People who fall under this particular category, whether male or female, both tend to display an enormous amount of confidence, mainly in their appearance and status, yet when you take time to get to know them, you'll find that they lack in substance. They don't challenge you, nor themselves, they tend to be ok with where they are in life but talk of big things. This generation has lost focus of the true meaning of love, we've lost sight of what it means to truly love ourselves, we lack in knowledge of loving people, yet we excel in the area of loving materialistic things. What good is it for us to love things we won't care about a year from now, clothes we won't be wearing months from now, yet, take for granted someone who's been there for us, who's held us down who has shown genuine interest in us, even on the worse of days.

Now, I know many may be wondering how is it I know so much about "f" boys and girls? Well, I've fallen in this category at one point. Grant, it, I was younger but I too went through that stage of being a "f" boy. Those were the worse days of my dating life. *"Honest moment"*. The sad part is, I sucked at it, it was too tiring. I was pretending for the linkings and acceptance of people, who didn't even care much about me to begin with. I only had one thing in mind when dating or pursuing a woman. Yep, that's right. That was me. I played the game and lost, I've caused hurt, pain, confusion, disappointment. Then I found myself being the recipient of my own weapon I had formed against women. I knew what was happening as it was unfolding, so I couldn't be mad, I had to take it like a man, realize that it was a lesson I had to learn. It's so easy to exert a high confidence level when nobody knows you, but when you try doing so with someone who actually knows you, you tend to look foolish, sound foolish.

There are two types of gentlemen who will read this book. The first, is one who's reading, or perhaps his lady is reading, with sound effects and looking at him and he's thinking to himself, I see where I can get better doing some things, or I see where I may have fallen short in some instances. For sure, I'm going to man up and get better. To that gentleman, I say, keep up the great work, you're on your way to becoming that man you were created to be. Now, there is another type of man who will read this book and think, "I can't believe Mike is telling all the secrets, card revoked" and to that gentleman I'll say, I understand, but somebody had to do it. You'll thank me in the long run.

What matters most is not that you're the perfect gentleman, but what matters most is that you're authentic, real, honest, true, loyal, respectful, driven and that you give your all to the things and people you love. That's what matters most. Notice, none of those things had to do with your appearance, on purpose. Many times, we focus on the outer, neglecting the inner, when the inner is what will affect the outer, not the other way around. The outer is important, don't get me wrong, we see a person before getting to know them, so how you definitely want to make yourself visible, by looking presentable. Remember, often times, how we're perceived will dictate the way we're received. You want to look your best as often as possible because you never know when time and opportunity will meet and you don't want to miss out on what or who could be there waiting and ready to meet you.

Now fellas, I understand we come from different backgrounds and have different upbringings, but let's step our game up and look like men. The way fashion is moving in is getting more and more feminine. I'm not judging your style, if that's what makes you happy, by all means, you go right ahead, however I am saying, a gentleman carries himself in a certain manner, which we'll discuss in the next chapter. What we wear tells people how we feel about ourselves, it causes people to think or try to determine, how we should be treated. If you don't believe me, next time you go somewhere, perhaps the bank, the grocery store, mall, club, or lounge, wear some jeans and a t-shirt and see how you're treated, perceived. Then go back a few days later, wearing a suit or perhaps some nice slacks and a nice shirt, button up or polo and see the difference in the way people treat you. The unspoken truth is that, people treat you differently, take you more seriously based on how you dress. A gentleman, is a gentleman not based on how he dresses but more so, his actions, how he carries himself.

Hopefully this will cause my fellow gentlemen to take a look in the mirror, become more self-conscious about how we carry ourselves, how we treat our woman, or how we treat women period. When we get our acts together, that will cause for our women to start believing in us again, believing that we can lead our relationships and families, that we can be depended upon, relied on and counted on, that we won't fail them, that we will, stick with our relationships regardless of how hard things get. To the "*f*" boy and the *"f"* girl, I hope you'll take this information in and allow it to begin to work in your life. Apply certain principles, beginning with "treat others how you wish to be treated" that's a great start for any self-improvement.

Truth is, we all have some pieces of "f" boy and "f" girl in us. So, no-one has room to judge you and what areas you should work on to become the best you. This is simply a challenge for us all to take a look at those areas we often try to cover up and ignore, the areas that aren't the most likable and work on bettering those things. Don't become better for others, most times we try to change for people, it doesn't work out the way we hope, but change for yourself, change because you want to be a better you, on the inside. It's easy to front and pretend and get people to view us a certain way whether it's accurate or not, whether its truth or not, whether we're overly confident, rather than actually being confident but move into the state of not only looking good, but actually being good.

"The Supreme Gentleman"

In this chapter I'd like to take a look at a rare breed of a man, he's not your ordinary man, he's not basic, he's extraordinaire, he see's life in a different way. He may have gone through his different phases of life, which have caused him to learn many lessons but in this moment, he operates in wisdom, uses intellect when he speaks, thinks before he reacts, he walks in confidence, yet he is humble. He has a love for God that he doesn't have to go around telling people he has, because they see it, they feel it. He's not after just any woman, but he loves a challenge, a woman who's about her business, who has balance in her life, or working towards getting it. He is *"The Supreme Gentleman"*. What makes up this man, it's a combination of things and in the next few moments we'll dive into details of who and what this man is all about. Let's first talk about the way he looks. He dresses sharp, to the T, regardless of the apparel, whether it's jeans, slacks, a suit, or even sweats and he always makes sure his hygiene is on point. It's not what he wears, it's the way he wears what he wears.

"His Mind"

His mind is what causes people to be in awe of him. He listens before and more than he speaks, but when he speaks, people listen, people pay attention to his words because he only speaks what's truth, what's wise, he speaks life. He's well versed in many things, yet he's not ashamed to admit he doesn't know it all. He's hungry for knowledge of those things he doesn't know. He's always spreading good and positive vibes to those he's around, whether a social or private setting, he doesn't just settle for the outline, he's into the details. When you meet him, ladies, you know there's something that's just different. His conversation excites you, draws you in and makes you want to know him in every way. He's business savvy, thinks out the box, whether it's innovative business ideas or things he's planning on doing for the sake of entertainment. You'll find yourself wanting to be close to him, not knowing why? Or what it is about him that has your antennas up, but you'll know it's just something, different from anything you've ever experienced and different from than anything you know you'll ever experience.

CHAPTER 5

"The Basics of a Gentleman"

I'm sure if you're reading this book, chances are you have an idea of what a Gentleman is. Being a gentleman is simpler than what one may think. We all know of the basics, hopefully, if not, it's ok, in this segment we'll dive into those basic characteristics a man can work to gain, or work on to improve that a gentleman should possess. Let me first say, the interesting thing about being a gentleman, is that it doesn't take funds for a man to possess these basic characteristics, Chivalrous, Courteous and Honorable. Many of us develop these at an early age, through parenting, we learn to open the door for a woman, if walking with a woman, be sure to be closest to the curb, ensuring she's protected on the inside, pulling the chair out for a woman at the dinner table, when speaking to a woman, showing eye contact, removing your shades, unless the setting causes for you to have them on. These are all acts of Chivalry, which after practice, becomes second nature. Now, in this day and age, those who don't understand, mostly in this and the younger generation will think it's weird, some may even snicker or laugh, but any person who is "woke" will understand. I'm speaking from experience.

I've been applying these characteristics to my life for years now and many of the women I've taken on dates are sensible women who have an idea of how they should be treated, yet they're still very appreciative of a man being a man, being a gentleman. I've received many compliments for my actions, which at this stage of my life, it's funny to me, because I only imagine it to be normal, but the reality is that its few and far in between. When you begin to walk in the light of a gentleman, people can't help but notice. Why not stand out for doing the right thing versus the wrong thing. If you want something different, the truth is, you must do something different. Don't go with what's the status quo, go against the grain of what this lost generation and what society tries to exploit as being cool.

A gentleman is a man deserving of much honor, regardless of the setting. Not because he thinks highly of himself, he's humble, yet when you're a gentleman it oozes out of your pores and people can't help but notice it. When he enters the room, whatever is out of order, falls into order. In his silence, he's demanding of respect, he doesn't have to yell to get his point across, yet his tone is firm, thorough, and sincere. He has respect for people, especially his elders, he answers with Yes Sir, No Sir, Yes Mam, No Mam. It's all about your mentality, that's what makes you a gentleman. It's so easy to fall into society's whirlwind of flawed definitions of what a man is or should be. I make it a point to purposely not fit in to any box that a person tries to put me in. Why be subject to their views? Why allow people's limited thinking of themselves, be placed on you? You have the ability and power to be better.

Being a man of honor, is probably the most important aspect of being a gentleman. People who respect you, look up to you, look to you, realize there is something special about you, that's felt whenever you're around. There's nothing wrong with displaying the greatness you have on the inside of you, especially if it's for the greater good. When people honor you, they'll go out of their way to be a part of whatever you have going on, because they've watched you. They have seen the way you move and interact with people, how you're comfortable in your own skin, you don't have to downplay anyone in order to shine, in fact, many times, you push people to do great things, to become greater. Think of those men in your life who deserve honor, perhaps it's a relative or role model you've met on your journey. What makes you give honor to them? Is it because they're relatable? Perhaps they came from where you're from and have made something great of themselves when others didn't. Whatever the case is, you look up to them, admire them for a reason and just as you admire them for whatever reason, people have a reason to admire you. The key is to find what that something is and share it freely.

"*The Supreme Gentleman*" is always looking for ways to

improve not just his, but the lives of those he's surrounded by. The goal isn't to just be great for your own selfish gain, when you're operating in a gentleman state, you become selfless, you begin to think of yourself less, not saying that you love yourself less, but your care for others will begin to be a priority. This is ultimately what makes that gentleman, supreme, his care for other people, his love for those in his circle and the way he treats strangers. It's not about self, self becomes small to fulfill the greater good of what God has predestined that man to be.

Ok Ladies, I know you're probably wondering, what about you all? How does this benefit you all? Well, now, that you know what to look for in a gentleman, his traits, things he should do as a man, as a gentleman, if you're currently dating someone, hopefully they fall into the gentleman category, if they don't, you can have that talk to try to get them to the point of striving to become their better selves. Any smart man knows that women have the power, some are just understanding of order and don't mind allowing a man to lead in the relationship. Ladies, it's important to allow a man to be a man in the relationship. I tend to date women who are independent, however I have to often times remind them, "You can save your independence when you're with me, I got you". Not to take anything away from you or your independence, nor am I doubting your capabilities as a woman, however, I am saying, I'm a man you can count on to handle business, relax, allow me to cater to you, I'm not too proud to ask for help, especially if it'll better our relationship and what we're building.

Fellas, gentlemen, don't be prideful all the time. I know we carry on this macho attitude and often times, if you're like me, you hate being wrong but we have to realize, women, the right woman is here to be our helpmeet. She's literally here to help us meet our best potential in every area of our lives. Out of all the women in the world, to know there's one woman, who God himself created for me, is mind blowing, excited, yet I often get nervous. When I think about commitment, not only to love her, but the commitment I make before God, on our wedding day, that's not something that should be taken lightly, and I think often times, people, not just men, but women also, fail to think about the seriousness of what we're doing."

The Supreme Gentlemen" thinks about that beforehand. Trust me, I know, having been engaged before, it was a big deal to me, but God said otherwise, which I was hurt, confused and even disappointed by but he knows best, and honestly, I can't say that my heart was 100% there. I gave 100% to our relationship but remember *"shawty"* who I mentioned earlier, well, when she was around, it was hard for me to give my heart to anyone else all the way. That's the sad truth. I'm grateful God orchestrated things to happen that happened, because I would've hated to have gotten to the altar or beyond knowing my heart was with someone else. If you find yourself in that similar situation, ask for direction, accept what comes. Often times we try to fight and change the will of God, which is the worst thing we could possibly do.

Now let's change the pace of things just for a moment because I can imagine, many of you ladies are asking yourself, how is **"*The Supreme Gentleman*"** in bed? Now, if you're not ready to find out, now is a great tine to skip this chapter. Let me first say, a gentleman is a gentleman even in the bedroom and his intent is to please, which many gentlemen, tend to be perfectionist in many different phases of life, the bedroom, isn't to be excluded from that. Actually, this can get so intense, it may deserve its own chapter. As a matter of fact, let's do that.

CHAPTER 6

"The Play Room, The Marriage Bed Undefiled"

It's been a long week, you're ready to get off work, because your co-workers have been pissing you off all week and you know you're seeing your man tonight. All day while at work, you've been checking in to make sure nothing has changed, he's been confirming plans are a go. Its 4:30pm and you rush out the door, get in your car, to get home. You pull up to the driveway and your man meets you to grab your bags and greet you with a hug and kiss, squeezing you tight, grabbing you're a** while tonging you down. He walks you up to the door and tells you close your eyes while he leads you into the door. You're wondering at this point what in the world is going on? He opens the door and you hear Bruno Mars **"Straight up & Down"** playing softly.

Once you get in the door, he tells you to open your eyes and when you do, you see the place is lit up with candles everywhere, rose pedals, leading to the bathroom, but first he sits you at the table while he fixes your plate for dinner. While eating dinner, you all begin talking about your day, but you see it in his eyes, his desire to have you, to want you, to please you, yet, he keeps his composure, relaxing and letting you eat. After dinner, he grabs your hand and lead you into the bathroom, once you enter the bathroom, more candles to offer lighting, the bath tub is nice and hot just the way you like it, with rose pedals sitting on top of the bubbles in the tub.

You finally get undressed and get in the tub, while in the tub, he begins to wash your body, while feeding you chocolate covered strawberries and you're enjoying a glass of wine. All while washing you, he can't help his hands keeps grabbing on you firmly, caressing your body, he can't help that his lips keep kissing you, can't help that his tongue keeps touring your body. Every moment getting aggressive, more intense, you're breathing begins to get heavy, his breathing begins to get heavy, he begins to squeeze you tight, he then gets undressed and joins you in the tub. He slowly slides in between your legs and begins to kiss you, while grabbing your neck, rubbing his hands across your cheek bones as he kisses you, he grabs you and leads you out of the tub into the playroom.

The Playroom, is where there are no limits, it's where the gentleman becomes the beast, ready to devour you, his beauty. The playroom, is candle lit, rose pedals spread throughout the room, incense burning giving a sweet aroma. The temperature is perfectly set, just the right amount of heat and air conditioning. The bed is made up of red silk sheets and black silk pillows, with plenty of throw pillows. He walks you to the door of the room, but before entering he covers your eyes with a silk sleeping eye mask proceeding to kiss your lips, then your neck, he grabs you tight leading you into "the playroom". When you enter the room, you first smell the sweet incense burning, he grabs you and throws you onto the bed, begins kissing your body beginning with your toes, leading up to your ankles, up to your knees. At this time, you can't help but think, how enraged your body feels in his hands, your entire body is now a portal of ecstasy, ready to burst with excitement.

He then pours oil on your body then proceeds to giving you an erotic massage and at this point, your body is now open to receive him. He ties your hands up, disabling you from being able to resist or fight off. He then ties your ankles, spreading your legs apart, proceeding to begin where he left off licking your calves, working his way up to your thighs, his tongue hitting all your secret spots that you didn't know you had, while grasping your waste tightly. Well, I think you can imagine what happens next. Come on, that's not the point of this book. Should I continue? Ok, okaay, I'll continue.

His moan as he tastes your sweet pearl, drives you crazy, he's licking and sucking your pearl causing your body to shake uncontrollably, you can't help but scream and moan, this man knows all your spots, how you love to be touched, kissed, made love to, leading you to climax, over and over and over, until you can't help but fall into a deep sleep. At least you thought you were, but he, this gentleman, can't help his desire for you, he can't help how bad he wants you, he's addicted to you. So, as you're asleep, he's holding you from behind and begins to kiss your neck as he holds you tight, working his way down to your back, making his way down to your pearl, yet again, causing you to be weak in the knees, he knows just what you like, the way you like it.

Hopefully, by now, you'll see that overlooking a gentleman, will cause you to miss out on an experience beyond your wildest dreams. Gentlemen often times get the stigma of being too nice, too sweet, friendly. While these characteristics are true, don't place a gentleman in a box, limiting him to what you think he is capable of. That is the wrong thing to do. Remember, a gentleman loves a challenge and won't back down from one. Just because he doesn't speak on or talk about the things he wants to do to you, doesn't mean he's not thinking about it. Timing is key, and a gentleman has patience, but when the time is right, he will make his move. Often times we rush into things before the time is right causing us to set ourselves up for disappointments. This is something both men and women have the tendency to do, mostly women.

Look, women are emotional beings, no, that's not a problem or a malfunction, however, allowing your emotions to get the best of you or ahead of you can cause you to make rash decisions. Think about the times you've rushed into something, just to find out it was leading nowhere. Don't allow people to put a time clock on your life. You may have your own time stamp even, but be realistic, how many times has life overturned your time stamp. You planned on going to college, finishing up in four years, you planned on being married and having kids at a certain age, even if you've accomplished those things, chances are, you didn't complete them in the timeframe you thought you would have. The beautiful thing about it, is it's ok, you're still ok and you have plenty of life to live. My thinking is, I'd rather take my time with finding the right person and getting it right the first time than to rush into a situation, only to have to start all over again. I'm not saying there's anything wrong with starting over some cases cause for a restart, or another chance, but why not be patient and really focus on you while waiting for the time and opportunity to bring you together with that special someone.

> *"It's better to do something right, regardless of how long it takes, then to do it fast and have to start over again"*

CHAPTER 7

"The Growth Process"

One of the most beautiful things I notice now and days is the push to become better from both men and women. If you were to log onto IG right now, chances are you'll see someone in the gym, bettering their physical, you'll probably see someone posting some motivational quote, inspiring change of their mentality, you'll see someone promoting themselves, their business, in order to better their social and networking environment. These things are great attributes to have in order for us to be pushed to the next level in our lives. I can appreciate social media outlets for those specific reasons. The harsh reality is for us to grow, pain is necessary. I've dealt with my share of pain; heartache and I can imagine many of you have as well. Life doesn't always make things easy for us, life tends to do the opposite, it's not easy. Navigating through life's challenges, phases sometimes can be brutal, truth be told, but the key, I've found out is choosing to become better, not biter.

I hear you thinking, "that sounds good" and it is good, at least it can be if you take on the right attitude. We've all heard the saying *"Attitude, determines altitude"*, which is correct. Whether it's your friendships, relationships, professional or personal, your attitude ultimately is the deciding factor of just how high you will go in those areas of life. You ever meet someone who has a negative outlook on life, where it seems there's always something wrong? They're always upset? Always pointing the finger at everyone else, never taking the time to look in the mirror at themselves? These are just the types of people to stay away from, especially if you're striving to move up in the world. Don't get me wrong, I get it, we all have our moments where we just feel down but at some point, you have to determine that you're going to change the way things are going in your life, decide that enough is enough, I'm taking control of my life, my time, protecting my piece of mind, surrounding myself with positive individuals who will speak life into me and my situations that don't seem to be in the best place.

Who handles heart break the worse? Men or Women? This has been a discussion and debate for quite some time and my personal opinion is that men actually do take heartbreak the worse. Please allow me to explain. It begins with the fact that men don't freely offer our hearts up, when we do decide to do so, typically it's because we feel that we can trust you and we do trust you. We go through a relationship becoming vulnerable, those things that we wouldn't normally care about, we begin to care about them, the hardness that makes up a man, begins to soften, the way our woman act towards us now has the ability to affect our entire day, mood. We give our time, our treasure, we've pursued, have taken you out on dates, gave you the password to our phone, well, that's a bit much, even If there's nothing bad in my phone, I'm not sure I'll freely give you my password. All of these things, while often times they're taken for granted, are big deals to men.

For good men, it's a hard time dealing with heartbreak, but strange enough, it's even more difficult for the *"f*** boy"*. Now, they'll never admit it, but in most cases a woman who's been faithful, kind, nothing but good to a *"f boy"* often times resort to a good man after, if they've learned their lesson and for a *"f boy"* to see this, is the worse. This is why anytime a woman is happy after a break up, the *"f boy"* tends to come back around, seeing if that door is cracked for him to try to sneak in. He'll do *"f boy"* things causing him to lose a good woman, then go through a process of hurting, which generally begins with denial. You see, he has a hard time dealing with the fact that he lost a good woman, this is the time that you see the subliminal memes on his IG or Facebook page. You see him talking about him quoting lyrics of songs that disrespect women and how he's about his money, f*** these b****es. We've all seen it and that sort of behavior doesn't just come from nowhere. Some men don't know how to deal with being hurt, these same men typically will do things to cause hurt in a woman's life.

Often times men forget who is the ultimate prize in

the relationship. Yes, we too are a prize, but the woman is the ultimate prize and any wise man will tell you that the woman is the star of the movie, if you're lucky enough, she will allow you to be the co-star. Yet a good woman, makes sure you shine bright because you're a reflection of her, as she is a reflection of you. I've always had the thought process of, why go through building the courage to approach a woman, then having many conversations via phone, in person, text, FaceTime, to get to know her, taking her out on dates, actively pursuing her, just to mess it up. I believe with the way things are now in the world, with the next option being at our fingertips, men aren't forced to chase or pursue a woman, the way men once had to pursue them. Women, have made it a bit easier to get their attention and time, whereas, prior generations, women weren't stuck up, but they were sure of themselves, what they wanted in a man. I also believe the values that were instilled in those women, dealt more with character, how to carry themselves as a lady, how to not be loose, to not give every man their eye.

Let's just be honest, with growth, pain does come and often times in ways that are unexpected from those we east expect it to come from. I'm sure you can think of a time where you've experienced hurt in a relationship. Recall the anger, disappointment, confusion that situation caused you. We're given two choices when we experience hurt in life, either we can become biter or we can strive to become better. Notice I said strive, because choosing to be biter doesn't take much work, choosing to be upset, angry, aren't things we have to try to be when dealing with an unfavorable situation. The situation itself will cause you to feel a certain way. The interesting part is, although you don't have to work at feeling these emotions, the process is draining.

Intentionally make the choice to not allow your situation to dictate your emotions but you dictate to your situation how you choose to feel. Deciding to become better Vs biter isn't easy, but it is the most rewarding. When you're faced with a situation that presents you with the option of being upset, angry, hurt, be honest with how you feel, even voice it to that person who may have been the cause of you feeling that way, then decide to become better from it.

I've gone through a series of events that weren't the most favorable, some hurt beyond anything I ever imagined to be honest. It took me some time, but I learned over the years that although the situation may be ugly, piss me off, upset me or hurt me, I have the option of reacting in a certain manner. Yes, I could react the way my emotions try to push me to react or I can pray for peace in the middle of that storm and believe God will come through on my behalf. Isn't it funny that many of the situations you thought you wouldn't be able to get over, make it through, that man or that woman that you thought would have a hold on you, you've been able to make it through, you've overcome.

In the storm it appears there's no way out, when in reality, if we just keep the pace and stay the course, there is always light at the end of the tunnel. No, it may not seem as though you'll be able to get over that man or woman but life has proven again and again that you can make it through if you believe. Imagine all the times, you thought you were deep in love and wouldn't get over that man or that woman, now, think about where you are in this very moment. Some have probably moved on to the one you're supposed to be with, getting ready to marry, some of you have probably moved on and enjoying the single life. Whatever stage you are at in the process, you've moved on, you've gotten over it, you've grown beyond that point.

Growing causes pain, as pain causes growing. Now I know that sounds like a contradiction but think about it. Sometimes we hold on to people who we should let go because we're afraid or don't want to realize how life would be without them. Some people have been in our lives so long, they have become a part of our routine schedule, we know when they're going to text, call or FaceTime us, we know they're schedules and they know ours. What has been doesn't mean or doesn't justify for their continuing to be any existence within that friendship or relationship if there is no growth, development, or connection. So many stay in relationships for different reasons which aren't enough to hold the relationship together. It takes more than love for a relationship to continue being a healthy one, flourishing one. Many people have stayed and stay together for the sake of allowing kids to grow up in a home with both parents. My question to those who choose to do that is, what's worse? A child growing up in a single parent home? Or a child growing up in a multi-parent home where love doesn't exist? They say kids feel everything, so don't think that they don't feel the absence of love present in a home.

I know of many people who stay together because they've been together a long time, mind you, I'm not speaking of married couples but boyfriend and girlfriend. For men, I wonder, why is it, if you truly love her, do you hold her hostage, never intending on taking the relationship to the next level? If you have a good woman, that's down for you and you know she's down for you, why not take the relationship to the next level. I understand that we all want to be at a certain place in our lives when we decide to get married, for some, being rich or wealthy, for some, years in your career or on the job, for some, making sure there's absolutely nothing better out there. Yes, men do that as well ladies. We know you all do it. If you don't intend on marrying her, yet you say you love her, love her enough to let her go.

For women, I wonder, why is it that many of you stick around when it's been years and he's still not talking or trying to take your relationship to the next level? Are you waiting for that great day of an awakening when he realizes that you're his wife? Or is it because you feel that you've worked so hard to get him where he is that you're ringing the alarm and you'll be damned if you see another chick on his arm? Yes, that was a Beyoncé reference. Back to what I was saying, why is it that you're sticking around? Some stick around just to save face and not have to hear the "I told you So's" from family, friends and others. Listen ladies, I get it, you want it to work with him, he's your type, fits your world, met your family, maybe he's met your kids and they've developed a relationship and you don't want to let him go because of them having a male figure in their life means a lot to you, but why prolong the inevitable?

We have to realize that while holding on, keeps us in a situation, that doesn't mean that it's a healthy situation. Think about it, you hold on to them because you've been together for five plus years, which becomes six plus years, for what? Just to say you're in a relationship? Just to be in a relationship? That's self-sabotage. If you know it isn't going anywhere, why hold on to a dead or dying situation? We must realize that holding on to something dead only brings hurt to ourselves and isn't worth it in the end. I've been in situations where I too have held on to dead situations and in the end, it caused me nothing but pain and hurt.

Let's dive in to the bitter reader, the one who's so angry at that person who hurt you, who you feel wasted your time, who played with your emotions, who's name just makes you sick to your stomach. Let me first say, what you're about to hear, you don't want to hear but you should hear it. I've been through it and the first step from being free, is to forgive them. It's not the easiest thing, but the truth is, it's the best thing to do. Don't hold on to the hatred, hurt you feel, that will only keep you held back from moving forward into your future. You can't truly move forward in life and love, until you've honestly closed the previous chapter. How do you know when that chapter is closed? The ill feelings you've had, you'll no longer have. You'll find yourself at peace with the situation, with the way things ended. When you run into them in public, while you may have this weird feeling, it's not hatred and that's the first indication that you've grown beyond that bubble.

CHAPTER 8

A Season Vs a Reason

In this life we come across two types of people, which, I'm sure we've all heard mentioned in speeches, sermons, quotes. There are those who come into our lives for a Reason and there are those who come into our lives for a Season. I'd like to pose the thought that some people's reason is to come into your life for a season. In this season, lessons can be learned, knowledge can be gained, self-awareness can be established, Self-Love can be manifested. We can go through life in fear or we can go through life facing our fears. Often, our best lives are what's waiting for us on the other side of fear. Think about the times you've been faced with something that made you nervous, that made you think twice before reacting, responding or moving into your next phase of life. When you decided to face that fear, was it rewarding on the other side? Did you come to realize it wasn't bad as it seemed? Did you come to see that you were afraid and fearing for no reason?

In Love, relationships, dating, sex, many of our fears come from previous experiences, things we've experienced, seen or heard. We fear failure, we fear giving our time to someone only for them to waste it, we fear opening our hearts to someone only for them to take it for granted, we fear laying down with someone only to find out they have been busting it open for the community, for lack of a better phrase, sleeping with many different individuals at the same time. We have many reasons why we have fears but when we learn to move beyond what we fear, there's a great reward awaiting us.

I'm not saying go out and start risking it all for the sake of Love, but I am saying you shouldn't allow fear to be the cause of you missing out on something or someone special. Being afraid with the chance of succeeding is far different with being afraid because you sense nothing good will come from a situation. Does he give you butterflies when he talks to you? Does she take your breath away when you look at her?

I've experienced being afraid to love someone, not because I was hurt or anything but the total opposite. Our connection was something that couldn't be put into words, we clicked in every area, we got one another and yet, I was afraid of loving her. That kind of love is out of your control. Men, I'm sure I'm not the only one but I don't like not being able to control my feelings for someone. Being in control always is important me. We're comfortable being the dictator of our feelings and love, wanting or desiring a woman, but a good woman, makes that extremely difficult. The truth is, we don't mind diving into the true being of a woman once we know for sure she's different from the rest or down for us. Especially now, dating has changed tremendously, where women tend to be the ones playing games, playing the game. Yes, ladies, it's true, while it may not be all of you, there are plenty of you who play the game, and so well, might I add.

Let's talk about the Seasonal individuals that come into our lives. More often than not, those we encounter on a daily basis, whether friends, co-workers, even relatives, are more than likely seasonal people. In the dating world, we get it wrong 99% of the time, yet the one time we get it right accounts for 100%. The 99% represent the individuals in our lives that are for a season of dating, getting to know one another and then eventually that relationship ends. It's important to realize the difference between the two. Those who are meant to be in our lives for a season shouldn't get lifetime treatment. Ladies, what I mean by that is, men will repeat what works as long as it works. When dating, no woman gets treated differently until we find that woman who stands apart as being special in our lives.

For a moment, think about the term "tricking" which is used to describe a man who spends frivolously on a woman, maybe by way of gifts, drinks in a club. Now, because of the way I date, I've been confused with being a trick, from the outside looking in, it may seem to be that way but what sets me and many men like me apart is the mindset we have when treating a woman, a certain way. A man who tricks, is doing just that. Say I'm in the club and I see a beautiful woman, perhaps, not even beautiful, maybe she's just sexy, she's thick in all the right places and I want to have sex with her? Now, a man who's tricking, will buy drinks in the effort to impress a woman with his generosity, hoping to get a smile, a conversation ultimately her number, all with the intent on smashing, having sex. He's not looking to wife you, or take you seriously, he's attempting to trick you.

I have to turn a corner which many ladies reading this book won't like. Women trick as well, even more-so now and days than men. With the help of social media outlets and filters, men are taking risk when getting to know someone online. In person, women trick as well, from makeup applied to the face, to the body suits that hold everything tightly together, even enhancing those parts men look at. Women who trick, do so with the intent of causing, or persuading a man to trick on them. People who trick fall into the 99% category. Tricking is everywhere and people, especially women, are the most fallen victims. From the streets, gangsters who pretend to be hard, yet are soft, in the church, from the pastors to choir boys, gospel and hip-hop artists, who are on the down-low, I believe this is the worse trick of them all.

I'm not in any way bashing gays, but I am saying that those who pretend for the likings or acceptance of people for their own selfish gain and use women in order to do so, are weak individuals. Making a woman believe their straight and love women when behind closed doors they like the same thing their lady likes, isn't right. The hurtful part is, those women who are victims of this scam, suffer scars beyond what any man can heal. I've seen it many times, I've heard many stories and I'm sure you know of someone who may have gone through or even still going through this type of trickery. The 99% category is alarming and even when you consider those who are closest to you, many of them fall into this category.

I've learned over the years not every woman is meant to be my wife, although they may possess wife potential, there's only one woman who God has created and set aside just for me. I'm a lover at heart, so it is often times easy for me to take a risk on love but the truth is not every person we come across is deserving of getting to experience us in those powerful ways. Not every person qualifies for the premium plan. There are many who only qualifies for the basic plan. People have to be time tested and proven before we just give them or show them our best. Revealing your greatness before a person is proven deserving or that they're able to handle it won't yield the results you want. Learning to hold back some and revealing your dopeness little at a time prevents you from wasting time. Those on the receiving end of us giving and showing how great we are, aren't going to be the one feeling let down or played in the end.

Everything in life operates in seasons and as we all have learned and experienced by now, seasons do change. While, this holds to be true, for some individuals, they come into our lives and can cause a season to last a life time. Think of those friends who have become family, some even closer than family, these are people who are in your life for a reason.

"A Reason"

Have you ever experienced loving someone that perhaps, you never thought you would or could love them in the manner that you do? Have you ever been so connected to someone that even without them saying a word, you know their thoughts? You know how they feel just by looking at them? Even when they fool the world with their smile, you feel their pain and hurt? Some people are God sent into our lives to walk with us through the journey of life. People are sent to our lives to walk with us in different aspects of life, whether it's business, community, outreach, ministry, health, financially, spiritually, each of these individuals hold a special place in our world and help to contribute to us becoming our best selves.

There is one person who God sends our way to be there every step of the way. That one person who we have an undeniable connection with that seems to never go away. This is typically the person that's on our minds last thing at night before we go to bed and even the first person on our minds when we wake up in the morning. This is the person that we ourselves willing to drop everything we're doing for if they need or just want our presence. This person feeds your soul, more than and before taking from you, they're always there when you need them or even when you least expect it. If you've never experienced this before, I hope that when you do, you're ready to receive it and I pray that you accept them. Don't make them pay for the mistakes of others. Realize they are wired differently and they weren't sent in your life to play games with you, or use you. They only require two things of you. One, that you continue to be you and blossom into the woman or man God created you to be and secondly, that you accept them for who they are.

Now, that you have that person in your mind, are you all together? What's keeping you from taking the step forward? Gentlemen, If you have this, I challenge you to not waste time looking to find it in someone else, because chances are you won't. Even if it begins to seem as though you've found a woman who you connect with, if she's not the woman God created for you, she won't be the one you're connected to. We can connect with many, but we're only connected to one. It's time we stop making wives just our child's mother. If you don't intend on marrying her, why sleep with her? Save yourself and her the trouble and headache and allow a man who will take her seriously to come in and love her.

Ladies, if you have this, what's keeping you from allowing what feels real to you, to your heart to manifest itself in your life? I get it, a man should be the one who pursues and leads the way when developing a relationship beyond friendship. I respect and understand you wanting to be pursued, as a woman, you should be pursued, sought after, chased. If a man isn't taking the steps and you've made yourself available, I'm not talking to you so much. For those of you who do have a man that you know your connection to him and with him is unlike anything else you'll ever experience or ever experienced, who is pursuing or attempting to take the relationship to the next level, yet you continue to keep him at bay or in the friend-zone, I ask, Why? Are you afraid of actually allowing love to love you? Is it because he's not your type? You can't find it in you, to love him or let him love you?

Whatever it is that's blocking you from experiencing love, if it's not something that goes against your morals, religion, if it isn't something that will cause you to change for the worse or become worse overtime, if you don't get disgusted when you look at him, if he's not your type yet you still find yourself attracted to him, then you can work to get past it. Do you not have faults of your own? Beautiful women, often times have the deepest scars. While beautiful on the outside, the attitude, the mood-swings, the spoiled behavior, the indecisiveness, can be a lot of baggage to carry and he's willing to carry yours, why not carry his. Often times women stand in their own way of receiving love, then wonder why it is they can't seem to find love. Well, perhaps love has found you yet, you're too caught up in your mind, and you own type that you're missing out on something or someone beautiful.

Many people miss out on the one who God has for them

because that person doesn't look the way they pictured in their mind. They don't fit the description of how they think love looks, never having experienced love. As I've matured my wants and desires in a woman have shifted past looks. Don't get me wrong, I believe my wife will be beautiful physically but more so, I pray for a beautiful soul, a conscious mind, a loving spirit. I pray she's business savvy and down to earth. I pray I learn to love her the way she needs to be loved and she learns to love me the way I need to be loved. Life has a way of showing us in time, who it's meant for us to be with, to spend our lives with, to learn with, to grow with, who's hear for a season, and who's meant to be here for a reason. We must be careful not to give seasonal people, lifetime benefits.

CHAPTER 9

Attached Vs Connected

For some, they spend their lives with someone who they're attached to, while others spend their life with one who they are connected to. Life has shown me that while we can be attached to anyone, whether by association, relationship, in the dating world, sex brings about attachments, but a connection, can't be explained, it is deeper than what we can explain, what we can even control in many cases. We go through life having multiple attachments, we get attached from hanging out or spending time with someone, being in a relationship with them, then we break up and when we break up, we detach ourselves from them.

Many relationships we have or have had, we were attached to that man or woman. We feel love, deep like, interest, we spend time getting to know them, we go on dates, pursue them, googley eyes and kissy face emojis, only to find ourselves reevaluating our relationship and realizing, we're not actually in love with them, yes, we love them, but we know it's not feeding your soul. I can honestly say out of all the women I've dated, the one I was connected to, wasn't my girlfriend, at least she's never held the title of such. I know I'm not the only one who's had a connection with someone who wasn't your actual woman or man, but there was just something different, something special that you felt, that you knew existed.

Attachments often take from you leaving you to question why? Or how? Why did I even bother? Why did I waste my time? Why did I ever trust you? How could you do me like that? How could you take me for granted? How could you do this or that? Attachments have to be detached in order for you to actually connect with the right person. We attach ourselves to people and situations that mean us no good, but perhaps they just feel good, we hang out and its cool, we guess, we settle for attachments because to connect requires work, it requires you giving up something. Marriages last when you're connected to that person. It prevents arguments and being afraid to communicate with one another. When we're connected to someone, they don't have to say a word yet we know exactly what it is they feel, we a look at them and know whether something is wrong. Being connected to someone, gives you dating super powers. Fellas, imagine being able to look at your woman and know that something is wrong, which is half the battle. Women want to feel that you care, they want to know you care about how they feel. It's not about saying you care, it's about showing you care.

Don't stop doing the things you had to get her once

you get her, but do more after you get her. Laziness, allows for the destruction of a relationship to take place. Don't be complacent once you've got who you've been pursuing. Men, we have to become more attentive to our woman, pay attention to her, get to know her and continue getting to know her. Don't get comfortable in your relationship, because relationships require work and there are no days off. Love give you the drive you need to continue to keep going strong for your woman in your relationship. When you have a connection, it makes everything inside the relationship stronger and better. Communication is better because you actually want to talk to one another, about the simple things, hard things, uncomfortable things. You become better managers of your money, you're able to come together to accomplish certain goals you have. You don't have to be stingy with your money but you're able to take care of business and save individually and collectively. Sex becomes a complete, spiritual, out of body experience. You remain attracted to one another which is key for success in the bedroom.

Have you ever experienced such a thing? Someone you're so connected to that you become selfless inside the relationship, what you want, begins to merge into each other's desires and needs, you're now in-sync with one another, operating on a higher level than that of the normal. We can experience the fullness of a relationship, but we must first learn to be open to it. It requires adjustments, giving up something for something greater to take place between the two of you. A true connection could lead to real, true love on a deeper level. Many people don't get to experience such a connection, many married couples today lack in actually being connected, yet remain married due to their attachment. Due to having kids together, purchasing a home together, living together due to the high cost of living. Whatever the case is, don't allow your attachment to cause you to be miserable. If you want something to change, you should be willing to change it. You have to be willing to become uncomfortable in order to get in position to receive something great. It's not the easiest thing to do but when you know you deserve better, you'll find peace in being happily single than in a relationship that you're settling for, just for the sake of being with someone.

One of the things I hate to hear is people say is "they mind as well marry this person because they've been together for so long". In many cases, this is a set up that can potentially lead to divorce. It basically says, I'm choosing to settle, I'm putting up with this person when it should be, I'm enjoying spending time with this person, I'm enjoying growing with this person, loving this person. Relationships should add to you, not take away from you, grant it, yes, it's give and take, but as much as you give, you should be receiving as well. When you're the one constantly giving, that can be absolutely draining, in any relationship but especially in dating, in building with someone.

For my young adult readers who are looking for something special, something real. When you find yourself searching or ready to find that special someone, look to find someone you can grow connected to and with, not just someone you become attach to. Attachments will keep you down, keep you from experiencing the supernatural. Sometimes we settle for the attachment due to us being afraid to move out of our comfort zones but it's when we choose to face our fears and move into the unknown that faith is activated. When faith is activated in a relationship that's when we're able to dive into newness of life, experience things that we would've never been open to experiencing while in our comfort zones.

Choosing to be attached to someone past time cause you to be drained, mentally, spiritually, financially, they seem to become a burden, rather than a blessing. This isn't healthy in any relationship. Dating someone should cause you to flourish. Ladies, men want a woman who will pour into us, build with us, connect with us. A woman who has asked me for very little, ends up getting everything and most men operate on this principle. When a woman has a give me, give me, give me syndrome, men shut down. A man who's searching for his queen, his wife, won't mind investing his time, energy, effort and money into her. If he sees you as such, you won't have to question his motives, he won't leave you guessing, he will be conscious in his decision.

If you ever want to see where a man's treasure lies, just watch where he put his money. Men don't just give our money to anyone, spend it on anyone. For those of you who desire a man with a nice size bank account, keep in mind, just because he has a nice size bank account, doesn't mean he's going to spend on or share that with you. Most cases unless you were there through the struggle, a man will be very stingy with allowing you access to his finances, that means, spending on you as well. Now, don't get me wrong, a ball player, entertainer, may be different, they may be able to spend without the thought of consequences and that's a beautiful thing if you end up with one of those. Let me challenge that desire for a moment, if I may. What's more honorable to you, a man who has millions and spends thousands on you, or a man who has thousands, or hundred thousand and invests thousands or hundred thousand in you? Many women will probably say, give me the millionaire, what's his is mines when we get married anyway. Well, if you weren't with him prior to him becoming a millionaire, do you not expect to sign a prenuptial agreement? I hear you thinking, I'm not signing nobody's prenup. Well, why? If you're marrying for the right reasons, with the right motives, it's a piece of paper, it doesn't say he's doubting you all will survive as a couple, however, should he not protect himself? Now, I'm just challenging those of you who's requirement involves millions in the bank account at the time a man approaches you. No man wants a bill in the form of a woman, he wants a woman who he can trust with what he has and trust she will do right by their union.

A good method for men to do is the $100.00 Test which I've conducted a few different times. Each time I conducted these test, they were out of the blue and I wanted to see exactly where their minds were. Grant it the first time I did it, I was much younger and so was she. So, as you can imagine she did what a young woman would do, she spent it, fast. Literally, handed it to her, she started cheesing, thanked me and drove straight to the mall to spend it. This showed me that she couldn't be trusted with too much and perhaps I'd need to be stingy with my funds, which caused me to become stingy with my time, which affected my effort leading to us breaking up and going our separate ways.

The next time I conducted this test, I was a bit older, a bit wiser and so was this young lady. We had been together some time and I felt things were getting serious but before taking the relationship to the next level, I wanted to see what she'd do with the money. I was in Los Angeles, CA where she was staying and It was for Valentine's Day. We had gone to dinner at WP24, we had a beautiful evening and the next day we were going out for her birthday. I handed her $100.00, she looked at me, smiled, and told me "no, you've done enough" while attempting to hand me the money back. Me being the type of man I am, I persuaded her to take it and do whatever she'd like with it. Well, while we were spending time that evening of her birthday, she looked at me and told me she couldn't wait to see me in two weeks, I looked at her confused, trying to recall us making plans for me to come back in two weeks, not that I had an issue with it, but in my confusion, I asked her what she was talking about? She smiled and said, "Well babe, you said do what I wanted with that $100.00 you gave me and I want you, here, so I got you a ticket back here in two weeks" all I could do is smile and think of how amazing of a soul she was. She showed me that I was important to her, that more than my money, she wanted my presence.

Each woman will do something different with that $100.00 and each just show you, what they think of you, if they think of you at all, if they're thinking futuristic, if they're thinking about themselves. Ladies, what type of woman are you? What would you do if a man gives you $100.00 and tells you to do whatever you want with it? Believe it or not, just the simple answer gives you a self-reflection of your overall character. Are you stingy, are you ready for marriage? Are you able to take a simple seed and plant it causing it to grow? Whatever your answer is, it's ok, no matter what people say or think about you. You are able to change, to mature and become who God created you to be.

We all have things we can work on becoming better at truth be told. For me, like most men, my pride and ego has caused me to miss out on different experiences with women. Many men die alone because of those two things getting involved in our relationships. Pride, keeps us from realizing the power in a sincere apology and effort to get better and not make that same mistake again. We've all heard the saying, put your pride to the side, which in order to win in life, in love, that's a key element. Just because you're a man and God calls for men to lead in their relationship, you have to be wise enough to realize that your woman isn't beneath you, no, but she stands beside you, you don't rule her, or run her, she allows you to lead the way, trusting you're following God. Ultimately a man who follows God leads himself and his woman's relationship into a blessed life together as well as individually.

A man who's not following God, has no real sense of direction. If you're following a man who's not following God, the two questions you should ask yourself ladies. The first, who is he following? And where is he leading you? The way you love your woman, should be a direct physical extension of the way God loves her. To love her the way he loves you, you must first see her the way he sees her.

The most powerful love is that of the love that God has shown he has for us. Now, imagine being able to see your woman the way he sees her, love her the way he loves her, care the way he cares for her. Loving her without any leaks or holes in it, but just a pure and genuine love for her because she's your woman, your queen, your lady, your wife, your treasure, your love, your baby, your boo thang, loving not just what she does, but simply because she is who she is. Learn to love her goofy things, her weird things, the small things she does just to keep being your eye candy, the big and extravagant things she does in order to show you she cares about you. Learn to be attentive to her and watch how she reciprocates and appreciates you.

A woman's love is the first thing any man ever knows, whether he realizes it or not. This would explain why we go from one woman who raises us and trains us as we grow up, being our mother and join another woman who accepts us, loves us, caters to us, build with us, take the little we have and multiply it making a beautiful life. Connecting to the right source, being the right woman, for a man, causes that man to mature, develop and seek what's greater out of life.

Now, ladies, just as men should be a direct extension of God in physical form when it comes to loving you, you all have the ability to be that to men as well. No, men don't need another mother, but a woman who has his back, who caters to him, who loves him, embraces him when she sees he's had a long rough day. For a hardworking man, peace is golden. A man who's worth your time shouldn't have to fight to love you. Loving you should come easy. Allow yourself to be loved by him and realize that we as men, desire to love you because loving you does something for us in return. It's in love that we become our better selves.

"It's easy to run, why not take the hard road and stand, be loved and love"

CHAPTER 10

Man Up, Woman Up, Grow Up

It's time for men to us gentlemen to become the kings that live on the inside of us. Yes, it takes time to become that, but with effort we can accomplish it. It seems that we're losing sight of the importance of family. We're making more baby mothers than wives, while children are a blessing, lets care enough to marry their mother and raise them together so they can grow up and repeat that cycle. The time for playing games is far gone, life is too short and we can't continue to take it for granted, we can't continue to take our queens for granted. Just because she's been down for you, if you have yet to put a ring on it, she has no obligation to staying down for you and now and days women are waking up to who they are and leaving.

Its time out for being afraid to be vulnerable, for a man who's not afraid to be vulnerable is a real man, a strong man and a brave man. I'm not saying just be soft, no woman wants that, however I am saying when you have a special woman in your life, you'll notice soft spots begin to develop, don't be afraid to show that to your woman an only your woman at times. Timing is everything so be mindful of when she needs to feel you're caring side, when she needs to feel you're loving side, your hard side. It's ok to take the cape off and be Clark Kent. You don't have to be superman all day long, she doesn't expect you to be that all the time.

Man up, speaks to those who have yet to cross over from the playing games stages. The thing about the game is that, nobody wins, only love wins in the end. You'll find yourself repeating the things you've sown, rather good or bad. Imagine, everything you've done to these women, to your woman, some man doing to your daughter. You're probably thinking, "I'll kill him". Well, why not kill that part of you that's doing those very same things you'll kill someone else over? That is someone's daughter as well, is she not worth being loved, cared for?

We have to put away those childish things, such as being a player, having meaningless sex with random women, having a woman who deserves to be a wife, yet keeping her attached just so no one else can have her. These are all childish things and are no good for anyone. I marble at men who do things to impress other dudes. I don't understand that mentality and I'm glad I don't. Men are players because they haven't found the one who has everything they actually want in a woman, in most cases. If you've found her, take her seriously and put a ring on it. If you're connected to her, pursue her with the intention of marrying her. No need for playing or wasting times. More than likely, she feels the same way yet, because she's a woman, with class, she will conduct herself as such and keep quiet until you make the first move, so make your move.

What makes a man isn't based on what he has between his legs, now and days, that can even be altered but more so what makes a man, a man is his mentality. How do you view the world? Do you value people or use them? Do you treat women with respect or go around degrading and disrespecting them, referring to them as Bi**es and H**s? Do you give back to your community, or are you making a difference in your community? Do you reach back and help the next man up when he's down, or do you laugh at him in his current state? These are the things that make up a man, but a gentleman, does these things and add to them.

Man Up!!!

Women, how do you view yourself? Are you a bad b**ch? Or are you a woman? A queen? Do you use men for what they can do for you? Are you a bill? Or are you a woman a man should invest into? You may have pearl between your legs and it may be good, but that doesn't make you a woman, a lady. Your mentality, how you view yourself is important. How you view yourself ultimately will be the way a man views you. Women have the ability to training a man how they should be treated. A man wants to capture you, win you, for you are the prize.

Many of you reading this may find yourself in a place of being tired. Tired of men playing games, tired of men coming in and wasting your time. Tired of holding a specific man down and him taking you for granted. Is that you? Or perhaps you're in a relationship that you've been in and it seems as though you're just stuck, you're attached because of this or that? Maybe you find yourself in a situation where you're in a "mind as well" type of relationship. You're just with them because you've spent so much time already with them. Well, to you I ask, twenty years from now, what will your excuse be? If you're tired of where you currently are, make the necessary change. You have to be willing to be uncomfortable in order find something greater or for that someone to find you. Proceed with caution of course but don't deny yourself from experiencing something beautiful.

It's time to realize the power you possess and operate in that. Don't waiver just because things haven't worked out in the past for you regarding love, that is the past. Accept what has happened, or what it is and make the necessary change. You have the power to change the way your book ends. Chapters come to an end, when it does, accept it and move on to the next chapter of life. Realize that the most beautiful experiences are yet to come. Take the negative experiences and transform them into positive ones. Queen up, rise up and keep building yourself, keep growing and blossoming into that woman God created you to be. Love will find you and when it does, this time, it will be real, it will be what you've dreamt it would be and even better.

Woman Up!!!

The gentleman seeks to love, a woman who's true to herself, who doesn't pretend for the likings of others or is concerned about what others think. A gentleman knows and doesn't deny his hearts desires. Only a fool does such a thing. In the journey of my seeking and looking for a queen of my own, I've found the many mistakes I've made in the past from moving too fast, just because it feels right, doesn't mean it is right or it's meant to be. You have to be patient in this journey to find who God has for you. It's not the easiest. I've dated some of the most beautiful women, with great personalities but they weren't for me, not forever at least. Being a gentleman is a steady walk, constant improvement is necessary, you work to master being a gentleman. We strive to become better each day, mastering one thing in a day, is a productive day. No one has it all together, at least if they're alive they don't, believe it or not we all have that something we're working on or perhaps should be working on to become better individuals. Both men and women have their struggles.

Have you ever noticed that some of the most beautiful, sexy women have the most insecurities? They begin to rely on makeup, speak about their flaws, the pimples that visit unexpectedly, their shape not being that coke bottle anymore, not knowing what to do with their hair. We see them and think, wow they're beautiful, they have this body that's banging, yet when you get to know them, you find out that yes, they may have this going on or that but in reality, they too are working to improve certain aspects of their makeup.

Beautiful women either go through life being told they're beautiful or they grow into being beautiful. Now those who go through life hearing they're cute, fine, beautiful, sexy, aren't impressed by a man saying it, unless she finds him attractive, they're more so use to it so hearing it from the average joe does nothing for them. The women who grow into their beautiful features tend to be more receptive of hearing those compliments, they come off a bit humbler than those who have heard it their whole lives.

As men, we also have our insecurities that we deal with. Our insecurities come from childhood experiences, roast, jokes from friends, rejection from women we want. I've had to grow past my own insecurities, being short and dark-skinned were always the highlight of jokes growing up. Those were the two things people, especially my brothers and my friends, always seemed to target when roasting me or clowning me. We know how ruthless and straightforward kids can be, my brothers, friends and I were no different.

I grew into being handsome, if I may say so myself, lol and I'm glad that I grew into it because from it, I learned humility, to be humble, to not allow compliments to go to my head boosting my ego. I learned the importance of being competent rather than being overly confident. Competence is the ability to actually do something successfully, where Confidence is the feeling that one can do something successfully with no action being taken. I know some good dudes who are just overly confident for what they're actually able to do. While confidence is important in the dating aspect, it's more important to not be overly confident and to practice actually being competent in areas you speak of or show confidence in.

In spite my flaws I had growing up, being short and dark skinned, I still managed to have beautiful girlfriends, I mean, I may have had a few questionable ones, but for the most part, I've had some success. I relied on those things I was competent in. I was good at sports and that was a known fact for anyone who knew me, I was talented so I showed competence in those areas. Confidence and competence to a woman is what looks and personality are to a man, one may attract a woman, but whether you're actually able to deliver, will actually be the deciding factor of her actually staying or committing. For a man, a beautiful woman may attract a man, but personality will be the deciding factor whether you're a jump off or whether he's trying to jump the broom with you.

Grow Up!!!

CHAPTER 11

"From Lemons, to Lemonade"

In this moment I'm thinking of a time when things weren't so great between myself and this special woman I was dating. I'm reminded of the hard times we had to grind through to make our relationship work. I'm reminded of the many obstacles that could've potentially killed what we had. Distance, having differences in opinion of what we wanted in our relationship, what we wanted our relationship to be.

I'm reminded of the many times, I tried to walk away from her and how it seemed life always brought us back together. This was a trying time for me, because I knew what it was that I wanted and I knew how far I wanted to take our relationship, yet, she also knew what she wanted and how far she was willing to go with me and it was two separate ways. We weren't seeing eye to eye and we were both standing our ground on what we wanted.

I wasn't happy about the situation as I'm sure you can imagine, this was difficult, she wasn't just some random woman, she meant a lot to me and I didn't want to lose her. I knew that a decision would have to be made at some point and to be honest, I dreaded having to make that decision. I valued our friendship, relationship but I ultimately knew, unfortunately we weren't growing beyond that point.

I found the will to deal with what the reality of the situation was and little did I realize how much power I was taking back into my own life by doing so. So often we allow people we love and care about to have power over us to the point where we can't see our lives without them. Sometimes, life will allow you to experience a love with someone that's meant to be just that, a experience. Beautiful as it may be, this doesn't guarantee it's meant to last a lifetime.

By letting go of a situation, or someone, we're allowing room for God to send the right person our way. First you have to be willing to let go, trusting not in your own will, but Gods will. My own will, caused me to go back every single time but trusting in God and asking him to help you move on, gives you the strength to move on.

After accepting reality, it's then that we're able to move on, not to the next person. In reality the next person you should move on to after a break up or after walking away from a serious situation is yourself. It's wise to take time to evaluate the situation, the things you learned about that person, about yourself, consider the things you should work on to better yourself at or with. You don't want to carry old baggage into a new relationship or situation.

Men, more than women often move on a bit faster

than they should, without taking time to grow from that previous situation, learn from it. We go from relationship to relationship never seeming to be able to get it right because we don't consider or think about what went wrong previously. We re-cycle the mistake which could be avoided if we pause, work on ourselves, mature in those areas then seek to find someone else. Some habits are harder to break than others. When you've been with someone who's allowed you to get away with certain things, do certain things, when you get with a woman who's not as forgiving or not as lenient, it's a hard time trying to get it right. So is it then the woman's fault? She's at fault for allowing things to slide, but every person is ultimately responsible for their own actions. We'd like to play the blame game but in reality, we are the ones to blame.

A man can change, but it takes him having the desire to do so. No woman can make a man change, nor can she convince him. Giving a man, an ultimatum won't cause him to change permanently. He will change for the moment or long enough for you to forget the reason you gave him the ultimatum in the first place. A man truly changes, when he decides to change in his heart first. I've been one who's had to change and I changed when I decided to change in my heart first. My ego caused me to lose out on someone dope, so I vowed to never let my ego get the best of me again. It wasn't worth it. It took some time for me to get back to my humble place. I allowed the fact that I was known from hosting events get the best of me, when in reality nobody really even cares about that. They only care when they're able to benefit from it. Thankfully, I was able to get back to my humble state, I was able to get back to the reality of things, for me, I'm nothing without God and it's because of him, I'm able to have any success at all.

I don't know what your thing is that you have to work on, that's preventing you or may have prevented you to lose someone or something good but I encourage you to work on it. Allow that to be a lesson to you and grown from it. You'll realize you've grown from it when you're able to go back and confront that person you may have offended, made feel a certain negative way and apologize for who you were then. This is a big sign of maturity and maturity is sexy. Lol Ladies, I know many of you hold tight to your independence and that's a powerful, beautiful thing, but also find the balance of knowing when to allow a man to love you and be a man.

We don't know what we need until we need it. The idea that we connect with someone who has been set aside just for us, I can imagine it's not just for likes on Instagram or the ohh's and ahhhs and compliments. When you connect with that special someone, chances are they have something you need that goes beyond the physical aspect. For women who say "I don't need a man", that's a premature statement. You have plenty of life to live and you don't know what you need until you need it. A man can come into your life and push you into your destiny, the right man I should say. He can come into your life and through him, you find your purpose. It's very much so possible. Relationships are all about a partnership, two people joining together to become one. It's numerically impossible and this goes against everything we've learned in school. How can two become one? Well, it takes some subtracting from self, It takes realizing there's something greater at stake.

For every bad relationship you've had and experienced, the one right man or woman, can cause you to forget about the pain you once endured. This is turning lemons into lemonade, Love has the ability to make this possible. It's not something that happens overnight. Many of us have experienced many situations that one would wonder how it is that we're still in the race to find love, how is it that we still desire to trust someone with our hearts? Life is full of ups and downs, don't let the downs keep you down when you have the opportunity to get up. Don't look at where you are now and give up on yourself, just because you don't see it working doesn't mean it's not working. Sometimes we wait on God when he's actually waiting on us, to make the next move, even when we don't see the steps, have faith and take a step anyway.

I've been afforded the opportunity to host many wedding receptions and witness the union of two people coming together to take the next steps in life together. The amazing thing is, every step in a relationship, a different person is revealed to us.

When we first meet someone, we meet their representative, just as if we're going on a interview, the person they meet in that board room isn't who they see in three months on the job. They meet our best presentation of ourselves in hopes that what we show them, they'll be willing to take a chance on. Just as in dating, we meet someone, and they meet our representative, our best presentation, in hopes that they'll take a chance on them, that we will take a chance on them. We begin dating and you begin to learn about them, they get to learn about you and the interest starts to either rise, remain, or dwindle. This is the probationary period in the relationship. They haven't made it all the way in, but they're learning you, they're learning to love you, what you like to eat, what your hobbies are, your passions, dreams, goals, ambitions, if you want kids, 401k plan, where your money is spent, saved. The dates you go on in the probationary period are vital to the relationship. You begin to learn the person, another layer is taken off of that man, another barrier from that wall is broken down from that woman, you really begin to see them for who they are. You begin to court one another with the purpose to marry one another, this is the dirty stage. At this point, the man shows the sides others don't get to see, this is where the woman truly speaks her mind and if you two can make it past this point, you have a good chance at making your marriage last.

Those I see getting married, I'm always too amazed, how at one point, they were strangers, who became friends, who saw enough in one another, not knowing who that person would become or working to become and they took a chance on each other's representative, allowed themselves to walk blindly not knowing, if this person was serious about them at some points, not knowing what the relationship would become and there they stand saying their vowels, waking up to the person they will spend the rest of their life with. The process is scary, but it's promising if you're willing to work at it. I see couples all the time, working, debating, disagreeing, but they continue to work. That's the beauty of it.

Men have hurt women, women have hurt men, this is the truth. We can progress, we can change the rate of divorce, by changing our mentality regarding ourselves, by changing the way we view the opposite sex. Accept the fact that we've messed up, we haven't been perfect. Both men and women have played games, both men and women have taken one another for granted. I wonder what would the world look like if we begin to see ourselves as Kings and Queens, if we begin to treat one another as kings and queens? I wonder if men were to begin to see women and treat them like queens, stop degrading them, and taking them for granted? I wonder what would happen if women begin to look at men as kings, not just another dude, or random guy, or as a tool, someone you deal with whenever you feel like it, but what if women began to treat men like kings.

Of course I realize my thinking may be a bit farfetched and unrealistic, blame it on my optimism. I also realize that it's not impossible for us to begin to reframe our thinking, many of you possible already treat and see the king in him or queen in her and for you, I say, your pretty dope. Now for those who see the other as less than, I challenge you to really open your eyes, your hearts eyes and begin to shape your thoughts about them. Often times how we feel about others is just an inner reflection acting out the way we feel about ourselves. As long as we have breath in our bodies we have the ability to change, to become better, to turn lemons into lemonade.

CHAPTER 12

"Risking it All"

The one thing that puzzles me is how many people say they want something but aren't willing to put the work in to obtain it, or keep it. We have dreams, goals, visions that we wish to make come to pass however nothing happens without your participation. In order for things to become a reality in our lives, we have to take the necessary steps to make them happen. We have to work, relentlessly on some occasions for what we desire to happen and we have to work just as hard if not harder to keep them alive. This goes true for any business we wish to own, any project we work on, any relationship we wish to have and maintain. We hear many stories of people who obtain something then within time, lose it. This can be cause by many things including, self-destruction, having a prideful or arrogant attitude, not knowing how to treat people. It can also be due to obtaining something before you're actually ready to receive it.

Imagine wanting, operating a business and not having

the proper knowledge of how to maintain it. Not knowing is ok, at a certain point, however there comes a time when knowledge or the willingness to learn should take place. These examples work the same with relationships.

Many men want something real, want something substantial, yet when it comes to putting actions where their mouth is, they lack in showing. This actually goes for many women as well, say they want something real, yet aren't willing to work for it. Yes, ladies, relationships require work on your behalf as well. You can't depend on a man to hold down the fort all by himself. That's unrealistic expectations, even if in the beginning he begins holding things down on his own, he's only human and eventually will get burned out. Relationships are give and take, often times requiring what seems like more giving than taking but when its real and you understand your contribution goes towards the union, giving becomes easier to do.

A man is supposed to be the provider in a relationship, is often times misquoted and the meaning, I believe, is misunderstood. The meaning of provider has changed significantly then what it once meant. To understand the meaning of a provider, what it means to be a provider now and days, we have to consider many things. First, comparing the way households were in prior generations, men were the bread- winners while many women stayed home tending to the kids and the overall home itself. While, women were well able to be independence, most were married at an early age and were stay at home mothers while the man went out and worked. Moving into today, women are more independent and many have just as good paying jobs if not better in some relationships.

I'm not the type of guy who would have a problem with my woman making more money than me, her money is hers, I'm still going to be the provider for our home. A secure man won't have a problem with his woman making more money than him, nor will he abuse that. It's the insecure men who don't want their woman making more money than them because a woman who makes more money, has the option to opt out of that relationship at any time and you can't control her.

A strong woman has the ability to make more money than her man, yet allow him to still be the man in the relationship. She's not going to downplay him just because what's on paper. What's on paper doesn't always account for bills being paid, hair being laid, nails being done.

There comes a time when we have to mature, beyond our own selfishness if we want to have a healthy relationship. We all have something we know we need to give up, the key is to be willing to do so. I get that some habits are hard to break but it's a process of getting better. We have to ask ourselves a few mirror imaging questions. What it is that we really want? How bad do we want it? What are willing to give up or change in order to obtain it?

You say you want her, but are you willing to give up, or as they say when you're getting married, forsake all others for her? Are you willing to break your habits of cheating, lying, failing to respond to the entire text message and not just a part of the text? Are you willing to make her a priority in your life? Are you willing to miss out on hanging out with your boys and spend time with her? Are you willing to become disciplined and put your f**k boy ways to the side for her? Are you willing to take a break from being a gamer and focus your attention on becoming a better man?

These are the things we should ask ourselves even before pursuing a woman who's intentions we know are to find something longterm. If you know your intentions aren't of the same caliber, then let her be, so a man who's intentions are the same as hers can come in and love her the way she desires. We have to make sure our actions line up to our words, what we say, we're making a constant and consistent effort to make happen. It's important to first be honest with yourself, consider where you are in life. Things may not be perfect, you may not have it all together but are you making the necessary moves to get things in order? Are you attending to your business? While I understand the struggle can be real when it comes to home ownership, are you putting yourself in position to one day become a homeowner? If you are like me, that's something I said I'd wish to wait on my wife to accomplish together. While I'm still waiting on my wife, I'm putting myself in position that when I do find her that's something we can move forward with, removing some of the hassle.

I know many women are enjoying the heart to heart with the gentlemen, but now I also know that just as men often have similar things we need to work on or give up, women too have your things you should ask yourself before allowing a man to enter your life with hopes of building with you. Please note, these are just a few of the things us men notice many women struggle with. Are you willing to allow a man, not just any man, to lead the relationship? Are you willing to give up or forsake all others? Are you willing to curve all those fellas in your DM's (Direct Messenger) on Instagram? Are you willing to slow down from watching your reality tv shows that you love? Are you willing to make him a priority? Are you willing to add to his life in those intangible ways such as being his encourager, partner, shoulder to lean on when times get rough in his life?

I notice many women often times bad mouthing men for not doing this or that. The harsh reality is that a man will only do what you allow him or what he's been able to get away with while dating other women. So who's really to blame? Those previous women he's dated, him or both? Well, I can sense you thinking both. Well, lets not play the blame game, that gets us nowhere.

Whether you're a man or woman, the truth is, we all have our own things to get straightened out, we all have things to work on, even after finding your soulmate and getting married. Marriage is where the full time work begins. No, I'm not perfect and I don't know it all, but I do know that love is best when it's done right.

A Letter to Her

To you, beautiful queen, amazing woman, who's beauty leaves me speechless, I first say, thank you. Thank you for allowing me to be a part of your world, to play a small role in your movie. Thank you for allowing me to love you, to care for you, to appreciate you. I realize that any man could have been so blessed, and I'm grateful to God, he's allowed me to love one of his daughters. You are one of Gods most valuable treasures he's allowed this earth to have. I only wish I were over exaggerating, but the truth is I love everything about you. I love your voice, your laugh, the way you fall asleep at the drop of a dime, the way you never know what you want to eat, the way you know me so well, at times, to the point that it scares me. Often times I imagine in heaven, God was sitting there creating me, he looked and realized he still had the best piece of clay that wasn't used, and from that clay, he molded and molded, and he formed you. Perhaps I'm overthinking a bit, but the truth is our connection is so strong, it's as though I knew you, even before I met you.

I realize that I haven't been the best. I've failed to really see you, I've taken you for granted at times, I've failed to value your time. I haven't always cared, loved, the way you needed to be, deserved to be. You deserve to be loved each and every day, not just on holidays, birthdays, Valentine's Day, but every day. For this and so many other things, I may have said or done, I am so sorry, I apologize and I pray you can forgive me. You are the woman I love, I desire to spend the rest of my life with, you are who I dream about each and every night, you are the woman I care about more than anything in this world.

As much as I would love to promise to give you the world, the world isn't mine to give, but what I can promise, is that from this day forward, I'll treasure you, I'll love you, I'll show my appreciation to you, what you do for our home, our family, our kids. I can promise that you can count on me to be the man that you believe in, that I'll continue to follow God as he leads me, so I can lead us into purpose for our ministry, being marriage.

Any woman who's ever been hurt by one of us,

A Gentleman who speaks for gentlemen

About the Author

Michael "Mike Anthony" Holland is truly the modern-day gentleman with an old school soul. As the Owner of Plush Entertainment, Michael is geared to hosting red carpet events that change the mindsets of young and wiser adults regarding the night life in the Bay Area. Michael "Mike Anthony" Holland was born and raised in Oakland, Ca but it was in Atlanta where Michael grew the love for hosting events that cater to the mature, grown and sexy professionals. Aside from hosting, Michael is also a songwriter and producer.

Each summer Michael works with the youth in his community through the "YMCA" program, teaching young men gentlemen etiquette classes. Michael was inspired to write Lessons from a Gentleman through his own lessons he's gone through, experienced and began to share on social media outlets. It was there many encouraged him to write a book. This book is considered one of many to come that will inspire, encourage and spark conversations across the globe, regarding dating, sex, love and relationships. Michael sums up his life as being God led, Oakland Bred, and ATL Fed. In this it's his hope that you'll enjoy the reading and discussing this and other books to come.

Printed in the United States
By Bookmasters